# THE Devil Delivered

# THE Devil Delivered

## STEVEN ERIKSON

Introduction by Paul McAuley

PS Publishing 2005

## FIRST EDITION

The Devil Delivered
Copyright © 2005 by Steven Erikson

Introduction
Copyright © 2005 by Paul McAuley

Cover art
Copyright © 2005 by Edward Miller

Published in March 2005 by PS Publishing Ltd
by arrangement with the author.
Second printing April 2005
All rights reserved by the author.

This book is a work of fiction. Names, characters, places and incidents either are products of the author's imagination or are used fictitiously. Any resemblance to actual events or locales or persons, living or dead, is entirely coincidental

**ISBN**
1 904619 14 2 (Paperback)

**PS Publishing Ltd**
Grosvenor House
1 New Road
Hornsea, HU18 1PG
ENGLAND

**e-mail**
editor@pspublishing.co.uk

**Internet**
http://www.pspublishing.co.uk

# Introduction

by Paul McAuley

Although *The Devil Delivered* is an end-of-the-world story, it's by no means the kind of old-fashioned catastrophe still peddled by Hollywood, in which the Earth is threatened by a single, easily understood threat—an asteroid, or a plague of ambulatory plants, or giant flesh-eating bunny-rabbits. Something that can be blown up or slaughtered or reversed in a last-minute effort by heroes who are cheered to the rafters when the world emerges from its bunkers, blinking in the light of a brave new dawn. In this vividly-written novella, the threat is to the human race is the human race itself, and Steven Erikson refuses simple heroics, and refuses to simplify the hydra-headed consequences of total environmental collapse caused by over-exploitation of the biosphere and the rest of the Earth's resources, but confronts them head-on.

The catastrophe is all-encompassing. As in the dystopian visions of John Brunner, notably *Stand on Zanzibar* and *The Sheep Look Up*, the spew of information needed to plug us into the happening world can't be contained by ordinary narrative; its converging stories are augmented by tickertape updates, excerpts from newsfeeds, and a Greek chorus on a clandestine internet bulletin board. In the territory of the Native American Lakota tribe on the plains of Saskatchewan, as in the rest of the world, everything is breaking down all at once, a locust-swarm of calamities large and small. One strand of the story chronicles environmental destruction inflicted during the twentieth century; another describes the deepening conflict between the Lakota, who have an audacious plan to heal their land, and a brutally repressive economic bloc; in a third, a scientist observes extraordinary adaptations by plants and animals to a poisoned landscape drenched in ultraviolet light that burns through the ragged ozone layer. Slowly and certainly, they converge on an extraordinary moment of expiation and transformation.

I have to confess that just about everything I know about Steven Erikson has been googled from the internet. Formerly an archaeologist and an anthropologist, he's written a brace of contemporary novels and enough short stories to fill two collections, has previous form in the PS novella series, and is currently just over halfway through a ten-volume Big Fantasy series, the *Mazalan Book of the Dead*. But while *The Devil Delivered* just sort of landed in my lap, I'm more than happy to talk it up. Not only because its powerful story revolves around a bunch of my own obsessions, including post-colonial politics, dead zones, ecological collapse, and panspermia, but also because of the focussed intensity of Erikson's tough but ultimately hopeful vision, and his confident fusion of past and future, fact and fiction.

As more and more of what we used to think of as science fiction becomes science fact, there's a growing trend for sf writers to retreat to the golden futures of the genre's past, to retrofit good old-fashioned futures in which technology is a gift that's not double-edged, and geeks can still inherit the Earth, or indeed the entire Universe. I confess that I enjoy a lot of this stuff—I've even written some of it—but I also worry that if the entire genre turns its back on the real world, if it refuses to grapple with the events and ideas that shape the times in which it is written, it's in danger not only of losing its edge, but of entirely dissolving into misty nostalgia. It's in danger, like any organism that can't adapt to changes in its environment, of becoming extinct.

Many of those old-fashioned futures, the slide-rule dystopias, engineers' wet-dreams, and Gernsbackian emporia of technology, inhabited by men and women as bloodless as their machines, were unreal because they were not rooted in reality. They were as sterile and idealised as the gated suburbs to which the middle-classes retreat when they perceive that the centre of their city has become too dangerous; anywherevilles that, tailored to the commercially-driven aspirations of its purchasers, attempt to shut out the rest of the world because the world is messy, confused, complicated, and full of human mistakes. Easier to erase or ignore all that; easier to introduce some kind of gap or memory hole, a disjunction between the past and present of the story; easier to start over with a blank sheet of paper. Easier, but not better.

Like the best science fiction writers, Steven Erikson knows that if stories about the future are to be truly believable, they must be built on the solid foundation of the past, which is of course our present. And like our present, like the kind of science fiction that's the hardest to write, the near future in *The Devil Delivered* has been utterly and irreversibly shaped by its past. Like these early years of the twenty-first century, it clangs with the sound of the bills for the sins of the last century being paid in full. That's what its characters must deal with before they can move on; that's why it's crowded with literal and metaphorical ghosts. A windstorm strips dirt back to glacial gravel, and reveals that a farmhouse has been built over that staple signifier of accursedness in modern American horror, an Indian burial ground. The man-made mass extinction event of the present is echoed by the slaughter of the plains buffalo in the nineteenth century, the extinction of American megafauna in the Pleistocene after the arrival on that continent of human hunters (Erikson is robustly unsentimental about our ancestors; as one of his characters puts it, no savage was ever noble), and a deeper, darker event buried in a secret history of human evolution.

Ghosts and decidedly weird secret histories—although much of its story is set in the near future, and although Erikson scrupulously details the human agencies that wrecked the Earth's biosphere, *The Devil Delivered* is not exactly in the mainstream of science fiction. A former farmer believes that angry spirits were loosed when his father ploughed up American Indian holy land, and must be appeased; a messianic scientist is guided by an actual ghost (the ghost of Custer's nemesis, Sitting Bull, no less); some of the science, including fast-forward evolutionary adaptation to extreme environments and a radical rewrite of human descent, is more X-Files than actual. This isn't a bad thing. Gregory Benford once said that writing really good hard science fiction is like playing tennis with the net tightly strung; that is, by playing your game within the strict limits of what is known about the way in which the universe works. Erikson, dispensing with that net, is playing another ball game entirely—something as fast and intense as squash or pelota. He blends his gonzo bricolage of science fiction, fantasy, and horror motifs into a seamless whole that crackles with energy and is dense with information and ideas.

And most importantly, he founds his story solidly in reality. The environmental ruin and catastrophic extinctions of *The Devil Delivered* are what could easily happen if we don't begin to clean up our act at once; they could happen anyway, despite our best efforts, because they're already happening. We're in the middle of the greatest extinction event since the demise of the dinosaurs. Catastrophe is part of the weather report at the end of the evening news. It's in our blood and our bones. Steven Erikson's powerful, angry, hopeful story shines a brave light on the encroaching darkness.

*Paul McAuley*
*London, October 2004*

# THE Devil Delivered

"And the Word was made flesh,
and dwelt among us..."


Would you leave this place then,
where bread is darkness,
wheat ill-chance,
and yearn for wickedness
to justify the sternly
punished;

would you hold the driven knife
of a tribe's political
blood, this thrust of compromise,
and a shaman's squalid hut
the heart of human
purpose;

would you see in stone the giants
walking the earth,
besetting the beasts
in dysfunctional
servitude, skulls bred flat to set
the spike—

would you flail the faded skin
from a stranger's flesh,
excoriate kinship
like a twisted flag from bones,

scatter him homeless in a field
of stone;

where tearing letters from each word
stutter the eye,
disarticulating skeletal maps
to uplift ancestry into ageless
lives, progeny schemes are adroitly
revised.

Bread is darkness,
wheat ill-chance,
and all around us
wickedness waits.

*vii) tall boy*

# Prologue

Entry: American N.W. Aut. B.C. 8675 +/– 600 yrs.

Larger shadows walk with the coyote, elder cousin ghosts panting the breath of ice.

He watches them, wondering who will speak first. The coyote seems a likely candidate with its nose lifted and testing the air. Human scent riding the wind, now fading, slipping beneath the overwhelming stench of sun-baked meat, its touch on canine olfactory nerves an underscored sigh beneath the old scream of death.

The coyote pads down the slope, winding a path round the dusty sage, pauses every now and then to read the breeze, cock its ears in search of wrong sounds, scanning the low bluffs on the valley's other side, then continues its descent.

He watches the coyote, waiting. It might be the ghosts will speak first. It might be that, after all. They're big, bigger than he'd thought they'd be, more than shadows as they slip closer, moving stretched and tall, shoulders bunched and heads swinging as if conscious of crowding tusks—a hunt long over, a hunt less than memory. But it may be that their days of remembrance are over.

The coyote is close now, and he can read its life. Like others of its kind, it has adopted a band of humans. It follows them in their wanderings, down onto the flats where the grasses grow high; and when the giant bison migrate north to the forest fringes where the bitter prairie winds are slowed, frayed by the trees, the humans migrate with them. And in their wake, the coyote.

The animal clings to their scent, sometimes seeing them but always at a distance. The animal knows its place—at the edge of the world, the world the humans now claim as their own. The world, reduced to a piece of flesh.

The stench hangs heavy here, in this valley's dry basin beneath cliffs. Here, where the humans have made another kill.

The coyote pauses, ducks its head and sniffs the trampled, red mud around its paws. It licks blood-soaked grass. Behind it, the shadow ghosts pace nervously, hearing yet again the echoes of competition, the battle they lost long ago. Still, the carpet of dead is welcome red...

He smiles at the coyote, smiles at the ghosts. He stays where he sits, among the thousand-odd dead bison that have been driven, by a band of seven humans, over the cliff's edge. Here and there around him, evidence of butchering on a dozen or so animals, most of them yearlings. Some skinned. Others with their skullcaps removed, tongues cut out from their mouths, eviscerated. A sampling of biology, enough for seven humans. More than enough, much, much more than enough.

Bison antiquus. Bison occidentalis. Take your pick.

A breed above. Ghost cousin shadows of the smaller bison that now cover the lands. Born in an age of ice, once commanding the plains, grazing among mammoths, giant sloths, horses—beasts whose time had ended—and now, with this final kill, so too ends the time for the giant bison.

Punctual as a cliff's edge.

Smiling, he watches the coyote crouch down beside a gutted bull and feed. One last time. A world emptied of bison antiquus, barring a holdout enclave in the forests north of the Winnipeg River.

He sees them now, all around, more ghost shadows, dull herbivores, shoulders bumping. And at the herd's edges: the coyote's dark kin, the cautious breed of Dire Wolves. Other predators in the beyond, others who ran out of prey at human hands: lions, short-tailed bears, smilodons.

It seems, then, that he is the one who must speak first. "Among the world's killers," he whispers.

The coyote looks up, fixes grey eyes on him.

"Among the world's killers," he says again, still smiling, "only us humans seem capable of seeking and finding new animals to hunt, new places to flatten underfoot in a jumble of bones. An accurate observation?"

The coyote resumes feeding.

"Oh sure," he continues, "you've an alacrity for adapting, there on the edge of our world. And your human host is far away now, well into their rounds. Does being so far away from them concern you?"

The coyote downs a mouthful of flesh. Flies buzz around its muzzle.

"After all," he adds, "their scent's growing colder by the minute, isn't it."

The coyote doesn't bother looking up, just shrugs. "No trouble," it says. "I need only test the wind, and find the smell of blood."

A good answer.

He sits and watches the coyote feed, while around them the shadow ghosts howl at the empty sky, the empty land. In those howls, he hears the kind of smile reserved for shadows lost to the world. A smile he shares.

# One

TO JOHN JOHN FR BOGQUEEN:
  Out of the pool, into the peat. Found something/someone you might want to see. Runner 6729.12 for the path, just follow the foot-steps moi left you. Ta, lover boy, and mind the coyotes.

---

Jim's story:

Saskatchewan, Dominion of Canada, 9th August, A.D. 1959

Bronze flowed along the eagle's broad wings as it banked into the light of the setting sun. Jim's eyes followed it, bright with wonder. His horse's russet flanks felt hot and solid under his thighs. He curved his lower back and slid down a ways on the saddle.

Grandpa had clucked his Palomino mare ahead a dozen or so steps, out to the hill's crest. The old man had turned and now squinted steadily at Jim.

"What do you see this time?" Grandpa asked.

"It's just how you said it'd be," Jim answered. He remembered what his grandfather had told him last winter. There'd been a foot of wind-hardened snow blanketing this hilltop, and the deep drifts in the valley below had been sculpted into fantastic patterns. They'd covered the six miles from the farm in the morning's early hours, jogging overland and using the elk-gut snow-shoes Grandpa had made the day Jim had been born, nine years past. And he remembered what Grandpa had talked about that day—all the old, old stories, the places and lives that had slipped into and out of the family's own history, on their way into legend. Batoche, Riel, McLaren and the Red-Coats, and Sitting Bull himself. It was the family's Metis blood, the old fur trade routes that crossed the plains, and of course the buffalo. All a part of Jim now, and especially this particular hilltop, where heroes had once gathered. Where they had talked with the Old One, whose bones slept under the central pile of stones.

Jim let his gaze drop and scan the space between the two horses. The pile remained—it had barely broken the snow's skin last winter, but now the hub of boulders threw its lumpy shadow across the west half of the Medicine Wheel, and the rows of rocks that spoked out from it completed a perfect circle around them.

"Who Hunts the Devil," Grandpa said quietly.

Jim nodded. "The Old One."

The wind blew dry and hot, and Jim licked his parched lips as Grandpa's blunt French and Plains Cree accent rolled the words out slow and even, "He was restless in those days. But now... just silence." The old man swung his mount round until the two horses and their riders faced each other. Grandpa's weathered face looked troubled. "I'm thinking he might be gone, you know."

Jim's gaze flicked away, uneasily studied the prairie beyond. The sun's light was crimson behind a curtain of dust raised by the Johnsons' combines.

Grandpa continued, "Could be good for wheat, this section..."

The boy spoke slowly, "But that'd mean ploughing all this up—the Medicine Wheel, the tipi-rings—"

"So it would. The old times have passed, goes my thinking. Your Dad, well, soon he'll be taking over things, and that's the way it should be."

Jim slumped further in his saddle, still staring at the sunset. Dad didn't like being called Metis, always said he was three-quarters white and that was good enough and he didn't show his Indian blood besides. Jim's own blood was even thinner, but his grandfather's stories had woken things in him, deep down inside. The boy cleared his throat. "Where did your grandpa meet Sitting Bull again?"

The old man smiled. "You know."

"Wood Mountain. He'd just come up after killing Custer. He was on the run, and the Red-Coats were on their way from the East, only they were weeks away still."

"And that's when—?"

"Sitting Bull gave your grandpa his rifle. A gift, because your grandpa spoke wise words—"

"Don't know how wise they were," Grandpa cut in, then he fell silent, his gaze far away.

Jim said nothing. He'd never heard doubt before, not in the telling of the stories, especially not in this one.

After a long moment filled only by the wind and an impatient snort from the Palomino, Grandpa spoke on, "He told Sitting Bull that the fight was over. That the Americans would come after him, hunt him down. That the White Chief couldn't live without avenging the slaughter—that the White Chief's justice counted only with the whites, not for Indian dogs. Sitting Bull was tired, and old. He was ready for those words. That's why he called them wise. So after McLaren arrived, he took his people back. He surrendered, and was starved then murdered. It would've been a better death, I think, if he'd kept his rifle."

Jim straightened and met his grandfather's eyes. "I don't want this ploughed up, Grandpa. Maybe Who Hunts the Devil is gone, but maybe he isn't. Maybe he's just sleeping. If you wreck the Medicine Wheel he'll be mad."

*11*

"Your father wants to plant wheat, Jim. That's all there is to it. And the old times are gone. Your father understands this. You have to, too."

"No."

"Once the harvest's in, we'll come out here and turn over the land."

"No."

"It's empty, you see. The buffalo are gone. I look around... and it's not right. It'll never be right again."

"Yes it will, Grandpa. I'll make it right."

The old man's smile was broken, wrenching at Jim's heart. "Listen to your father, Jim. His words are wise."

---

Val Marie, Saskatchewan Precinct, 30th June, Anno Confederation 14

William Potts opened his eyes to the melting snow puddled around his hiking boots. He rubbed his face, working out the aching creases around his mouth. A smile to make people nervous, but it was getting harder to wear.

Slouched in an antique chair and half-buried by his bootsuit, he turned his head an inch, to meet the eye of a diamond-back rattlesnake probing the glass wall beside him. An eye milky white, the eye of a seer proselytised limbless and mute, but scabbed with deadly knowledge all the same.

The aquarium sat on a stained oak end-table, its lower third layered in sand and gravel. Stone slabs crowded the near end. A sun-bleached branch stripped of bark lay in the centre, angled upward in faint salute. At the far end, two small buttons of cacti, possibly alive, possibly dead—hard to tell despite the tiny bright red flowers.

The snake was avoiding its tree, succinctly coiled on a stone slab, its subtle dun-coloured designs pebbled by scales that glittered beneath the heat lamp.

William watched its tongue flick out, once, twice, three times, then stop.

He grunted. "We are rife in threes."

At the crowded basement's far end Old Jim rummaged through a closet, his broad hunched back turned to William.

"This guy's eyes," William said, frowning at the snake, "are all milky white." He lowered his voice. "Time to shed, then? Tease off the old, here's something new. Into the new where you don't belong. You know that, don't you? Because your sins are old."

Old Jim pulled out a walking stick, a staff, and dropped it clattering to the floor. "It's here someplace," he said. "I hid it when that land claim went through. Figured Jack Tree and his boys would swoop down and take everything, you know? The snake's blind, son. Burned blind."

William shifted in the narrow chair. "Conjured by thy name, huh? Makes you easier to catch, I suppose." The snake lifted its head and softly butted the glass. Once, twice, three times. "One day," William told it, "you'll wear my skin. And I'll wear yours. We'll find out who slips this mortal coil first." He shifted again and let his gaze travel over the room's contents.

Old Jim's basement was also the town museum. Thick with dust and the breath of ghosts. Glass-topped tables housed chert and chalcedony arrowheads, ground-stone axes and mauls, steatite tobacco pipes, rifle flints and vials full of trade beads. White beads, red beads, turquoise beads. Furniture shaped by homesteaders' rough, practical hands filled every available space. Cluttering the walls: faded photographs, racks of pronghorn, elk, deer, heads of wolf, bear, coyote, old provincial license plates from before the North American Confederation, quilts, furs, historical maps. A fossilised human femur dug out from three million old gravel beds that, before the Restitution, would have been called an anomaly and deftly ignored.

William smiled. "Three million, ten thousand years of history jammed into this basement, Jim. Exactly where it belongs. In perfect context. In perfect disorder. With a blind snake curating the whole mess."

He ran a hand through his unkempt brown hair. "This stuff ever been catalogued, Jim? Diligently recorded and filed on dimette, slipped into envelope, envelope sealed and labelled, inserted into a storage box, box stacked on other boxes, shifted to a dark, deep shelf beside the rat poison, behind the locked door in the university basement a few hundred miles from here? And you presume the guise of science? Hah."

Old Jim didn't answer.

Answers are extinct. "I'm an expert on extinction," William said. "A surveyor of the exhausted, the used up, notions made obsolete by their sheer complexity. It's a world bereft of meaning, and who knows, who cares? I don't and I do. The last gasps of a dying science. The last walkabout, the last vision quest. We've digitalised the world, Jim, and here I am riding the sparks, in bootsuit and eyeshield and sensiband. Out under the Hole."

"Got it!" Old Jim straightened. In his hands was a rifle. He grinned at William. "Right after Little Bighorn, Sitting Bull ran up here to hide out from the Americans." He hefted the rifle. "This was his. Used it against the 7th. Left it behind when he went back to get killed. And you know what he said?" Old Jim's eyes were bright.

William nodded. "He said, 'The ghosts are dancing.'"

Old Jim shook his head. "He said, 'We have fired our last shot.' That's what he said. And that's why he left it here." Old Jim stepped close and placed the rifle, reverently, in William's hands.

William ran his fingers along the barrel's underside until he found the maker's mark, then he straightened and held it close to the aquarium's lamps. "English all right. So far so good."

"That's gone down the family line, you know? Hell, my family goes back to before Batoche. Metis blood." He removed his baseball cap and ran his forearm along his brow. "It's Sitting Bull's rifle, son, sure as I'm standing here."

"The stock's been carved some," William said. He handed it back, then rose. "You might be right, Jim. Couldn't prove otherwise."

"Some of you fellas should come down here and record all this stuff," Old Jim said. He returned the rifle to the closet. "Jack Tree gets his hands on this and you and your university can kiss it all goodbye."

"I'll suggest it to my employers," William said, pulling on his gloves. He paused, glancing at the rattlesnake.

Old Jim said softly, "Most of them gone now."

William nodded.

"Burned blind, you know. Can't hunt, can't eat. Fulla tumours and stuff, too. 'Course, not much left to eat out there anyway. Sure you don't want a hot chocolate?"

"Can't. I'm fasting."

The old man shook his head. "A damned strange thing to be doing, son, if you ask me. Exactly what kind of research you into?"

"I'm cataloguing ghosts, Jim."

"Huh?"

"I walk on the winds, ride the snows. My heart beats in time with the ticking of stones."

Old Jim's eyes held William's. Slowly, he said, "You'd better get something to eat, son. Soon." He reached out and tapped the goggles hanging around William's neck. "And don't take those off out there. Even when it's snowing. Blowing snow and clouds don't stop the rays. Nothing stops those rays."

"Burned blind," William nodded.

Old Jim walked over to the aquarium and studied the snake. "Around here, years back," he said, "these fellas were called Instruments of the Devil."

"Yea verily," William said. "'And into the pit God casts all vermin, and into the pit shall they slither unending among the implements of history.'"

"Never heard that Scripture before," Old Jim said.

William smiled, then headed for the stairs.

Old Jim followed. He watched William pull on the goggles and activate maximum shielding, then raise the bootsuit's hood and tighten the draw-strings. "Back out in the Hole," Old Jim said, shaking his head. "I used to ride horses out there."

"The horses run still," William said. He faced Old Jim. "Keep squinting."

"You too. Mind the Hole, mind the Hole."

---

NET:
14.30.06 STATUS REPORT 00:00.00 GMT

Means:
Sea Level: +82.37 cm AMR
Temperature: +2.6012 C. AMR
Carbon Dioxide: +.06% AMR
Carbon Monoxide: +1.12% AMR
Methane: +.089% AMR
Nitrogen Oxide: +.0112% AMR
Organochlorine count: +.0987 ppm (holding)
Airborne silicia count: +1.923 ppm (holding)
Aerosol Sporco (volume) +367 AMR
Mare Sporco (sq.km): 113000 (Med.) (rising)
    86950 (Carib.) (holding)
    236700 (Ind.) (rising)
Nil Ozone areas (since 01.01.14):
    Midwest Hole: holding
    Arctic Hole +23416 sq. km
    Antarctic Hole: +3756.25 sq. km
    Australian Hole: +6720 sq. km
    Spawns: 24 (varied) (down 13)
Rad Drift Alerts:
    India (north)

Korea (south)
Bio Alerts:
    Ciguatera Epidemics (+1000s): 17 (holding)
    Retroviral General: 07 (+6/01.01.14)
    Ebola-16/Hanta Outbreaks: 112 (+7)
    Undifferentiated ISE's: 316 (+45)
    BSE/CJD/CWD composite index: 2.4b. Species Count: 117
    Malaria N. edge: +2.7 Lat.
    Suvara N. edge: +3.12 Lat.
    Cholera Count (/millions): 270
    Bubonic: 113 (14 known bioflicked)
    White Rash Deaths: 12.67
    Morbilivirus-B22 Closed Zones: 16 urban (+1)
    Transmutative Viral Count: 1197 (+867)
Hotzone Alerts Political:
    Pakistan/India (last nuke 07.03.14)
    Zimbabwe (closed since 27.05.13)
    Congo Republic (closed since 11.07.08)
    Rep. Lapland/Consortium Russia
    Georgia/Chechen Rep/Consortium Russia
    Iran (closed since 13.04.04)
    Iraq (closed since 22.11.03)
    Sinjo/Taiwan
    Quebec/NOAC
    Puerto Rico/NOAC
    United Ireland/Eurocom
    Israel/Assorted (no recent nukes/biochem WMD)
    Argentina (internal, last Bik flicked 29.01.13)
    S. Korea (closed since 15.10.07)
    Indonesia (internal)
    Guatemala/Belize/Consortium Honduras
    Ukraine/Consortium Russia (no recent nukes/biochem WMD)
Confirmed Dead Zones:
    N. Korea

Iran
Syria
Afghanistan
Colombia
California
Confirmed Dead Cities (excluding those in nations above):
Jakarta
Seoul
Hong Kong
Jerusalem
Cairo
Berlin
Sarajevo
Baghdad
Denver
Toronto
Old Washington D.C.
Refugee-related Minor Conflicts/Incidents: +103
Flicked Biks this month: 0
Flicked Biobiks this month: 2
Worldwide weather forecast: hot and sunny. Hey folks, looks like another balmy day out there!

---

NET:
Suppressed File Index (NOACOM) 219.56b
Subtitle: The Restitution
Category: Social Sciences
Subcategory: Biological Evolution/Paleoanthropology/Archaeology
Abstract: The record of anomalous finds began with the first generation of archaeological investigations originating in Europe in the 19th century. Prior to a defined paradigm asserting an acceptable structure to human biological and cultural evolution,

many of these initial discoveries, subject to the same diligent application of accepted and then-current methodologies, were taken at face value and incorporated into the then-malleable formulation of said structures. The institutional and informal suppression of anomalous discoveries soon followed, at the expense of countless professional careers, and continued well into the 20th century and early 21st century.

Deep subsurface exploration for economic purposes repeatedly yielded unexplainable evidence of human presence at periods in geologic history deemed scientifically impossible; however, the academic and scientific institutions were securely entrenched and fully capable of suppressing said discoveries. It was not until A.C. 07 that incontrovertible evidence was uncovered in Cretaceous gravel beds at the Riddler Site in west Antarctica (for a composite list of evidence, cross-referenced dating techniques, and excavation report, see SFI NOACOM 222.3a), proving conclusively that the accepted evolutionary scheme for homo sapiens was in dire need of restitution.

Current theories on this issue—

Tracking...
Captured.
Rabbit goes back into the hat. Nada folks!

---

Entry: American N.W. 30 June A.C. 14

Outside, the wind, born somewhere out west, gusted through the small town with a howling hunger. Drifts of snow banked walls and stretched serrated ridges across the streets. Leaning into the wind, he trudged toward the hotel, its three-storied bulk barely visible.

Through his goggles the world was monochrome. White sky, blending with white earth. Patched here and there with the dark, angular bones of civilisation. Nature erases. Nature wipes clean the slate. Snow, the rough and wild passage of spirits. Glaciers, gravid with desire. He paused and looked up. Medicine Wheels spun up there, echoes of Ezekiel. More of them now, trying to tell him something in their blurred spinning through the stormclouds.

He pushed himself into motion once again. He passed a humped mound of snow. A car rusting under it—he'd seen it the day he arrived. A monument to fleeting technology. Once new, masked in wonder and promise. When in use, mundane, banal. Then forgotten. Now buried. The makers move on, unmindful of the lessons beneath their feet. Nature erases.

He headed up Main Street. The western horizon had come close, come to the town's very edge, a curtain of nothingness behind which things moved, things paced, things stampeded, things watched. Every now and then their shadows brushed the curtain. And beyond them, out on the snow-laden prairie, dead earth was marked here and there by boulders, boulders set out in circles in which other rocks ran in narrow lines, inward like spokes, and a central pile marked the hub. Medicine Wheels, not yet launched skyward, remaining earth-anchored with a purpose sheathed in silence, locked in antiquity.

The wind reached through to sting his face. Flesh-clothed people had lived out there, once. When the sun was just the sun, the sky just sky, long before the poisons and volcanic ash burned holes in the air. They talked with stones, made places where they and the ghosts could meet, places where they could dance.

A figure slipped out from an alley ahead, stopped to wait for him. The snows spun through its body, the wind whipped unimpeded by its hide cloaks and beadwork.

"I wonder how much you anticipated, old fella?"

The figure shrugged, melted in a savage gust of wind.

A stranger. An other. Not his kind, not his blood, not what he was looking for. An emanation curious, maybe, enough so to come for a closer look. Not there for answering his questions.

Not there for the civilised art of conversation. Hence, making a point.

"Thus did God, burned blind, reach down through the white, featureless void, and then did He touch the stones, and read them like Braille." He walked past the spot where the ghost had been, then crossed Main Street, heading for the hotel. "And He spake, and He said 'Behold these instruments of the Devil, that would give voice to the lie of the firmament.'"

His vision preceded him into the hotel bar, plundering lives—a half dozen regulars, old men and women whose farmland had withered and who now lived on government assistance, ignoring the resettlement incentives and urban start-up grants. The cities held nothing for them—nothing they wanted, anyway. And meeting every afternoon at their regular tables beside the frosted window that looked out on Main Street, they found the comfort of familiar faces and familiar stories, and the demons of loneliness stayed away for a while longer.

"Behold, I went out to withstand thee, because thy way is perverse before me."

---

NET: the swamp

CORBIE TWA:
    Oops! Where dat come from?
JOHN JOHN:
    More interestingly, where'd it go?
BOGQUEEN:
    What are you talking about? The SFI file or the quasibiblical dart?
CORBIE TWA:
    The quasiwhat? Those files show up alla time, Bogqueen.
BOGQUEEN:
    What's with the enunciation there, Corbie?

**CORBIE TWA:**
Colloquial program, girl.
**JOHN JOHN:**
Which helps the trackers fix you, Corbie.
**CORBIE TWA:**
Sure thing. I may sound like I gotta Confederate flag in my bedroom, but it don mean I live in Ole Arkansas, do it?
**JOHN JOHN:**
Where were we? We were here, I think. I've caught whispers about this Restitution thing. It's not easy breaking into those SFI's, you know.
**BOGQUEEN:**
It's the Track .12 entries that interest me, John John. It's a mobile, isn't it? Not easy to hide with one of those. But he's managing.
**CORBIE TWA:**
For how much longer, though? Anyway, there's no end of foo-stuff out there. Why pay attention?
**JOHN JOHN:**
Because the boy's playing in the Midwest Hole, right, Bogqueen?
**BOGQUEEN:**
It all comes with what you put together. Try paying attention to the shivers on the vine, Corbie Twa. There's weird things going on.
**CORBIE TWA:**
T'ain't nothing new with dat, girl. My weird meter's set very high, you know.
**JOHN JOHN:**
Extinctions. Anyone tallied the count lately?
**CORBIE TWA:**
I hate atavistic bastards—didn't know I knew big words, did you?
Anyway, who tallies anymore? Who keeps lists? Pictures in books, as far as my kids are concerned. Stuffed carcasses in

museums, test-tubes in freezers. Jus like the dinosaurs, John John.

BOGQUEEN:
Extinction's a fact of life, right Corbie? Hail the official line.

JOHN JOHN:
So, coyote ghosts and ancient buffalo. Curious.

CORBIE TWA:
Probbly some effed-up terrorist mystic with a fieldbook and too much peyote.

BOGQUEEN:
But he's slipping the trackers. That takes some doing.

CORBIE TWA:
Or an inside line. Some kind of NOAC counter-culture creepy.

BOGQUEEN:
Seems clunky. Too obtuse. Likely he's running loose.

CORBIE TWA:
Lil good it'll do im. Who's listening?

JOHN JOHN:
Picked up a squiggly from someone named Bound for Ur. Wasn't tethered.

Seems there was a spetznaz inc. incursion somewhere in Lapland. Went sour and nobody came back out. Any shivers?

CORBIE TWA:
Don't mess with the Lappies. Not a sniff. Sounds bizarre. A run on radioactive reindeer meat in Con-Russia. Those mafiboys like their meat.

BOGQUEEN:
News to me, too, John John. I'll check my sinkholes, though.

JOHN JOHN:
My tally list includes coyotes.

CORBIE TWA:
Make the road-runners happy.

JOHN JOHN:
    No, they're extinct, too.
CORBIE TWA:
    Bummer.

---

William entered on a gust of wind, the snow swirling around him as he turned and pushed shut the heavy door. He removed his goggles and blinked, waiting for his eyes to adjust to the gloom. Pool balls cracked and rolled, followed by voices off to his right. He untied the hood's draw-strings, unzipped his bootsuit.

A gravelly voice called out from behind the bar to his left. "What did I tell you, College Boy?"

William shrugged. "Seemed the genuine thing," he said, heading over to the counter.

"Damn right," Stel said, lighting a cigarette. Tall, heavy, late thirties, the hotel's owner leaned on the counter and blew a lazy stream of smoke in William's direction. She grinned, cleared her throat. "Didn't Old Jim tell it?"

"Yep."

Stel set a bottle of filtered water in front of William. "See, my memory's none too bad, eh?" She glanced over at the regulars and nodded. "Sitting Bull's rifle, sure as my ass is fat."

Laughter exploded in the room, forced, too loud.

William took a mouthful of water and swung his gaze to the pool table. A local boy was having his hands full playing a tall man in expensive clothes, a man even more out of place than William.

Stel bantered with the regulars, the old Indian jokes making tired rounds.

"My twenty-third Sitting Bull rifle," William softly sighed.

"What's that, College Boy?"

"Nothing." He watched the tall man circle the table once before dropping the eight ball on a called shot. Game over.

Behind the bar a phone buzzed. Stel snatched it up. "Yeah?"

A fingertip stroked William's shoulder. He turned.

"For you, College Boy," Stel said, leaning close. "Been thinking of closing up early," she added in a low voice.

"Sounds bad for business," William replied, "but good for the soul," he added as he took the antiquated phone. "Hello?"

Through an electrostatic crackle came Administrator Jenine MacAlister's voice. "William? Glad you're still in the town. The storm's supposed to last another two days—I didn't think you were that crazy, but I couldn't be sure."

"I am research incarnate, Dr. MacAlister."

"You didn't need to apply for an independent grant, you know that, don't you? I mean, we would've funded you, of course."

"What's up?"

She hesitated. "Something. Maybe serious."

William walked away from the bar, taking the phone and the water bottle with him. He sat down at a table tucked into a secluded corner of the room. "Go ahead."

"Well, I'll make it simple. Here's what I'm looking for, William. There may be some, uh, activity down there."

"In Val Marie?"

"No, no. Out under the Hole."

MacAlister's voice was pitched low. Excitement and conspiracy. Used to be a good anthropologist. Used to be. Now, just one more social engineer in an army of social engineers. Now it was games, cloak and dagger.

"What kind of activity?"

"The Lakota. They haven't been in dialogue with us since the Autonomy Settlement, of course, but we've picked up a hint of something."

Us and we. Defined exactly how? Us whites? We the Feds? The good guys, the cavalry? William's gaze fixed on the tall man at the pool table. "Haven't seen any around. Last I heard, Jack Tree was paying a state visit to Argentina."

MacAlister laughed. "It's not him we're worried about, William. He's had his fifteen minutes at the Supreme Court, and that was seven years ago. Come on, we both know who's about to take over the Lakota Nation."

"Daniel Horn?"

"That bastard is up to something. And it has to do with the Hole."

"Well," William said, "they own the land under it—"

"That's not the point. Hell, they've never forgiven us for that. As if we knew the Hole would open up when we gave them the land."

William's eyebrows rose. Gave? Jack Tree stood up against the Supreme Court of North America and tore that piece of ground right out of Fed hands. William massaged his temples. Medicine Wheels in the sky.

"In any case," MacAlister continued. "Have you seen Horn around?"

"Nope."

"Well, he's supposed to be in the area. Keep an eye out for me, will you?"

"My journal entries are available on the Net."

"Yes, William, but no one can understand them. I'd like something more direct, more responsive. One more thing, could be connected. There's rumours going around that the Lakota are about to close their borders. If you run into Horn, see what you can suss out. But carefully, okay? Don't push it. We'll talk soon, then. Bye, and good luck."

William climbed to his feet and drained his bottle of water. He walked back to the counter and set the phone down.

"Still planning on heading out tomorrow?" Stel asked.

"Yep."

"Well," she smiled, "I think I'll keep your room clean and ready, just in case you come to your senses."

William smiled back, then headed over to the pool table. The tall, well-dressed man was racking the balls for a solo game. The local boy sat at a distant table, looking glum. William leaned on the table and picked up the cue ball. "Finally," he said, "some competition."

"I'll break," the man said.

William dropped the cue ball into the man's hand. "Mother wants me to do some spying for her," he said.

Daniel Horn nodded. He walked around the table and set down the cue ball. "It's a hard life, William, and you're harder than most."

William found a cue stick. He raised one end and sighted down it, pointing the tip at Daniel, as if holding a rifle.

Leaning on the table for his opening shot, Daniel paused. Their eyes locked. "Careful," the young Lakota said, "that once belonged to Sitting Bull."

William lowered the cue stick. "She wants me to follow up a rumour about you closing the borders."

"You want me to tell you? I will."

"Nope. All I want to know is, open or closed, will you let me do my research?"

"That what you call it?"

"That's what I call it."

Daniel's eyes narrowed as he prepared to break. "Don't see why not," he said. A moment later the cue ball was a white blur, then a loud crack scattered the balls. Two thumped into pockets. Daniel looked up and grinned. "Better get out of that bootsuit, William, you're in for a hot one."

William shook his head. "I live in my bootsuit. It lives on me. We are one."

"Sometimes you scare me, William."

"Sometimes I mean to, Daniel."

# Two

Entry: American N.W. 1 July A.C. 14

Something heavier than an angel, something more like a witch, a woman of earth and stone—only this could have made her so tenuous to his touch. It is now an age of angels, gauze-thin and adolescent. But when he'd looked upon her face, something elder had been visible, a time abandoned in despair; he'd seen the solid anguish lining her face, and he made his smile soft as he let her into the room.

Sweat of the land between them, a smell of moss and cobble-cool flesh that he imagined alabaster and serene. Stel had left him with a gift, a warmth like sun-brushed wood taking root into what had been virgin soil. Not virginity of the flesh, but of the spirit.

Days since his last meal. Things out there crowding ever closer, eager to know this new stranger in the dreamtimes. What made the night important: he was already almost gone, wind-tugged away from civilised life. It could have been easy, to have just simply left, without a backward touch or glance.

One last time crawling out of his thermal controlled radshielding skin, once more unto the mortal coil. He thought then that a ghost stepped into him, a presence that understood the value of certain gestures to humanity—the one she'd give to him, the one he'd give to her.

A young man crafted by the tools of progress.
An ageing woman tired of sleeping alone.
Touched human.
Touched young.
"That wasn't pity," he said afterward.
"That wasn't bad," she replied.

---

NET:

CORBIE TWA:
    Somethin's cooking at Boxwell Plateau. Any shivers on the vine?
STONECASTER:
    Just this, Corbie Twa, the Argentinians made an official call to the Lady at Ladon Inc. NOAC got to them, goes the very soft twang. So maybe Boxwell's dead. And Ladon's homeless one more time. The last time.
CORBIE TWA:
    What about Saudi?
STONECASTER:
    You've been in the Swamp too long, mucker. Saudi was knifed a week ago. Now NOAC's got the embargo sewed up tight. Ladon can't even buy a scrap heap and a hamburger.
JOHN JOHN:
    This path ain't for gossip, muckers. Clear or get deep.
CORBIE TWA:
    Just fillin time, John John. Caught the last set of entries. Someone's slidin fast.
BOGQUEEN:
    Got a thing against sex, Corbie Twa?
CORBIE TWA:
    Seems a fall from grace.

JOHN JOHN:
>Corbie's got a thing, all right.

STONECASTER:
>Just don't know how to use it. Deep enough, John John?

BOGQUEEN:
>You wish, Stonecaster.

JOHN JOHN:
>The boy's about to wander, muckers. Running a varied call, can't be traced. All we've got is the American north-west. Big place.

BOGQUEEN:
>And a snow-storm, which places him on the north side of the Midwest Hole. The town could be Climax, Val Marie, somewhere around there.

CORBIE TWA:
>Climax? There's a town called Climax? Can I spend a week in Climax?

STONECASTER:
>So what's this boy of ours up to? Theories?

BOGQUEEN:
>Out under the Hole.

STONECASTER:
>Suicidal? What a disappointment. There's better ways, after all. Amuse yourself to death, it's what everyone's doing these days. I especially like the new Peasant Crusade. Imagine, dying at forty with a smile on your GO-FOR-IT-TILL-YOU-DROP face. All muscles and no fat makes Jack a dull boy, a dead boy.

JOHN JOHN:
>I doubt it's suicide. It's a quest of some kind.

CORBIE TWA:
>Oh no, a neo-pagan!

BOGQUEEN:
>Anything but. This boy talks the tongue of science.

CORBIE TWA:
> Really? I could've sworn it was soft porn with some hag named Stel.

BOGQUEEN:
> Can't wait to pick at your bones, Corbie Twa.

CORBIE TWA:
> Get in line, lady.

---

Lakota Nation, near Terminal Zone, 1 July, A.C.14

Behold these valleys of salt, and above, the sky of blinding white. Patches of nothing mar the world.

William darkened his goggles another setting and swung his attention to the snow-crusted valley below. A creek carved a route along the valley floor, slipping under old wood fence lines still tangled in barbed wire. Small twisted trees rose along either side of the creek, the branches thick with ice-wrapped buds.

He sipped lukewarm water from the spitter, clamping his teeth down hard on the plastic tube where it sat against the corner of his mouth. Behind him, near the tipi rings, his shield tent luffed in the steady wind, the sound like ghosts drumming on sand.

William watched two vehicles converging toward a low rise just above a bend in the creek. Their dark domes glinted dully in the afternoon's light as they crawled steadily like insects over the rolling terrain. After a moment, William rose from his squat and faced east. A half mile away the old blacktop highway stretched its way in a long, lazy bend southward. Terminal Zone, old Rural Road 219, a dead track reaching into dead land. Lakota Border.

He took another sip of water, shouldered his pack, then headed down into the valley. His boots crunched as he crossed a sinkhole where the day's heat had failed to melt the snow and ice. Elsewhere, the yellow prairie grasses shivered stiffly in the breeze, matting worn-down rises and rumpled hills.

A man had climbed out of each vehicle. They stood side by side at the edge of the creek and watched him approach. William waved. The taller of the two, dressed in the latest issue bootsuit, waved back. The other, old and bent and wearing a faded jean jacket, raised his head slightly, his mirror sunglasses flashing white, then looked away.

"Today's the day?" William asked as he strode up to them.

Daniel Horn slowly shook his head. "Your sensiband's flush, William."

"Almost sunset."

The old man gestured at William with a chopping motion of one hand. Without looking back, he said, "He doesn't care. He doesn't live under it."

William smiled. "And he that liveth seven score years shall no more fear God's wrath. Good afternoon, Jack."

Jack Tree chopped his hand a second time, turning to William. "I'll never show you the secret places, Potts. Never."

"I never asked."

"We were arguing," Daniel said.

William looked around, his grin broadening. "A private one, huh?"

"About you, William."

William pulled up his goggles and squinted until his eyes adjusted. He glanced at Jack Tree, then back to Daniel. "You closed your borders?"

"This morning."

"An empty gesture," Jack Tree said, shaking his head.

William studied the old man. The wind picked up strands of his long grey hair and tugged with steady rhythm. His hi-tech wraparounds looked snug and sleek and insectile. His cheeks were scored with deep wrinkles, the brown folds and black tracks mapping their own valleys, dry creeks and ridges.

"Hardly empty," Daniel was saying. "NOAC needs oil. Same old story. Fuel to keep the Pakistanis toe to toe with the Sikhs. The machine's thirsty, and the money men are sweating."

"Sanctions," Jack Tree said, facing Daniel at last. "It'll break us apart."

"No, it won't."

The two fell silent.

William reached under his absorption collar and scratched his neck. The material's osmotic qualities were fine for reclaiming moisture, but it felt like fire ants when friction heated it up. "What about my research?"

Jack Tree pulled off his glasses, his eyes sharp and black amidst a nest of wrinkles. "Research? Research your way back home, boy. This ancient land never belonged to you, no matter how hard you pretend."

William said, "I found a den yesterday. Three antelope inside."

Jack Tree frowned.

"They're fully nocturnal now. And smaller. Their front hoofs are spatulate, like shovels. Imagine that."

"The animals are gone," Jack Tree said.

William shook his head and smiled. "Just changing their old ways. Behold necessity and adaptive pressures, selection in all its glory."

"Is this your research?"

"No. But it's interesting, isn't it."

Daniel cleared his throat. "Like I said before, William, you do what you like. I'll tell you something, though. If peace and quiet's what you're looking for, you might end up being in the wrong place."

Jack Tree laughed bitterly. "Welcome to hell, then, Potts, and it's about to break loose."

"Old news," William said, snapping his goggles back down.

Daniel stiffened. "What do you mean?"

"Hell hath no fury like Nature scorned, Daniel."

Jim's story:

Saskatchewan, Canada, 19th July, A.D. 1972

Dust-covered cars and trucks crowded the farmyard outside the house. Everyone else was inside, neighbours and friends and relatives all circling Jim's mother, as if by numbers alone they could hold her there, in one place, forever.

Jim knew they'd say something if they could. They'd yell and show their rage, if they could. He leaned against his mother's Impala, rolling a cigarette. I can't blame her. I can hate her, but I can't blame her. Dad's slipping fast, only days left now. Metastasis, the doctors called it. From the bones to the liver, and still spreading. He already looked dead, doped up against the pain, withered by the months of chemotherapy. Three-quarters gone, one-quarter left and going fast.

He lit his cigarette. One of the barn cats had slipped out and now lay sprawled atop one of the herbicide drums lining the barn's wall. The cat stared lazily at Jim, then blinked and looked away.

The house door opened and Jim's mother stepped out, her cigarette dangling from her lips as she paused and fished for a light. For a moment Jim hoped she'd see him, and he reached for his lighter, but then she found her own and lit up. Pulling hard on her cigarette, she went down the steps, every line of her long, angular body stiff with fury. The door opened again as Grandpa and Ruth came out. Jim's heart jumped at seeing Ruth.

My wife. I'll never quite believe it. So beautiful, so solid, so sure of herself. And it was me she picked. Why? Why the hell why?

Ruth's green eyes scanned the yard until she found him. She shrugged: it's no use. She stayed on the porch while Grandpa joined Jim's mother. The old man spoke to her in quiet tones. Jim watched his mother nodding, her arms crossed tight against her chest. Smoke whipped in a stream from her face.

From the city. It had always been obvious. She'd only stayed because of Dad, and now he was dying, and her son was a man, married to a country girl which was right, and besides, all the words between her and Jim had been used up. The grief they shared was a chasm, impenetrably dark and too terrifying to cross. She wasn't staying. She was going back, where being alone wasn't quite so noticeable. I don't blame her. She's got her life, lots of years left. She wants to start over. I can hate her, but I can't blame her.

Ruth approached. "Roll me one," she said, sweeping strands of auburn hair from her face.

"Got some grass for later," Jim said, watching her mouth, wanting to kiss it and keep kissing it.

She smiled. "Not my style. You do the hippy thing."

"I love you, Ruth."

"I know." She leaned against the car beside him, their hips touching.

Three weeks married. All she has to do is get close and Christ, all I can think of is fucking her. Dad's dying, Mom's leaving, and none of it matters. Christ. He finished rolling her cigarette and lit it for her.

"Thanks," she said. Taking it from his fingers. They watched Grandpa and Jim's mother talking, there at the foot of the porch steps, the old farm house rising behind them. The curtains in the windows were drawn. To Jim, it had the look of a place waiting to be struck by lightning, waiting to burn to the ground, sending human souls flying skyward in a shower of sparks, a final release there on the trail blazed by his old man. Release, and relief. He realised, with a sudden thud in his belly, that he hated death, hated it like a person—with a face, a goddamned smile, gold-capped teeth, and eyes as deep as the flames of hell. One of the curtains moved. Elly, Dad's kid sister, peered out at the two talking in front of the porch. Her face withdrew after a moment, the curtain falling back into place.

"We'll be okay," Ruth said.

"I know. It's all right."
"Like hell it is, Jim."
"I know," he said again.
"It's not all right."
"No. It's not all right."
"But we'll be okay. Are you listening to me?"
He nodded.
"Don't hate her, Jim."
"I don't." But he did.
"She's earned the right. She stood by him, all through this. It was hell for her."
"For all of us. Grandpa's only son. My Dad."
"It's different. I know, you can't see that right now, but it's different."

He shrugged, wishing he wasn't so angry. "When I was a kid, Dad went and ploughed up some holy land. A Medicine Wheel, and tipi rings. There was a cairn in the wheel. A shaman had been buried there. A holy man. Or a devil, a spirit, or maybe both, one taking care of the other. Maybe there was a whole lot that was buried there."

"You think he's paying for it, now? Is that what you're thinking, Jim?"

He shrugged again, flicking the butt onto the dusty ground.

"Is that what your Grandpa says?"

"No," he admitted.

"Didn't think so." Now she was angry. It was a mood of hers that frightened him, because it left him feeling crushed, and that made him feel like he was weak inside. For all the outward toughness, he was weak—he prayed she'd never find out.

"You've been away," he said. "At school. Grandpa's not been himself lately."

"Are you surprised?"

He shook his head. "He's stopped talking about the old days. He told me it's up to me now to remember. So that's what I'm doing. I'm Metis. French and Cree, and it's the Indian part of me that's doing most of the talking in my mind. These days. It's, uh, it's the voice in my blood."

She was looking at him now, her eyes searching his face, or maybe studying it. She seemed to have shed her anger, but Jim wasn't sure what had replaced it.

"The voice in your blood?"

Suddenly embarrassed, he looked away. "Yeah. Sort of, I guess."

She was silent for a long moment, then she said, "Keep listening to it, Jim."

They both looked up at the sound of crying. Jim's mother was in Grandpa's arms. The stiffness was gone, and she looked almost child-like as she clutched Grandpa, her head buried against his shoulder.

"Christ," Jim gasped.

"Go to her," Ruth commanded. "Now, dammit. It's not just her husband she's leaving. Go on, Jim—you'll never get another chance."

The scene blurring in front of him, Jim lurched into motion.

---

Entry: American N.W. 1 July A.C. 14, Midnight

He lay in his tent.

And these lizards have gone reflective. Crusty, muricated, a sleight of sunlight shunting elsewhere as they hug their own shadows. Wondering at what's old about being new, the few generations of intense environmental pressures already forgotten except in the blood that threads their spines. And they hunt at night, amidst the hum and hiss of a thousand new species of insect in a hundred thousand iridescent colours reduced to grey beneath the moon.

He hides in his tent, reflecting. His skin has billowed out and is geodesic and is now crawling with many-legged silhouettes. He sees the lizards leap against his taut skin, jaws snapping. Exoskeleton crunches softly in the darkness.

Outside the lizards are feasting on St. John's bread, a mayhem banquet. And where is he, the one who giveth songs in the night?

A few generations of intense environmental pressures.

The Lakota hearths spread smoke haze across the plains. Seven generations lost in the wilderness, and now the eighth, rising once again, at last, rearing up and taking countenance of their ghost lands. The blood pumping from the ground has slowed, stopped. Somewhere vampires are screaming. The transport roads are barricaded now, the scattered small settlements isolated inside their rad domes, their skin taut and softly drumming to aborted intrusions from outside. Radio silence. The mute warnings of smoke signals unseen, unwitnessed.

They remain this night in their secret places, the past sitting in their laps like a child long overdue weaning. The old ones flinch and caress innocent's face, reluctant and angry at necessity's harsh slap. The young ones, who no longer recognise innocence at all, are brash and abrupt in their dismissal. For the old, the past weeps. For the young, the past walks, a mindful shadow anchored to the earth but facing the sky. The old reach for an embrace. The young are driven to dance. For each, the past obeys, as shadows must. Anchored to the earth, but facing the sky. And those shadows that weep, they are reflective.

"Read me then, for I am like Braille, and in the changing of my skin, something shall rise and find the stars."

The borders are closed, the lizards are dancing, the young and the old have met and argued, the antelope dig burrows in the false dawn, and the quest is now begun. And here where home is hell, the devil delivers.

NET:

CORBIE TWA:
> Oh my oh my. Possible? Accelerated genetic mutations in so little time?

BOGQUEEN:
> There's documentation to support it, especially among insects. As for the higher orders, who can say. The difficulty has to do with the sheer complexity of vertebrates. Speciation is rarer because so many more variables have to come in line for any major biological or behavioural traits to be expressed.

CORBIE TWA:
> Who ordered a text book? Look, our strange friend is talkin a maze. Has me wonderin if there's anything there.

JOHN JOHN:
> Watch the news, Corbie. The Lakota have shut everything down. NOAC's politicos are having a stock-tumbling fit. A team of multiculture negotiators is being assembled to discuss grievances, only the Lakota haven't voiced any. In fact, they're not talking at all.

CORBIE TWA:
> Multiculture negotiators? What the hell is that?

BOGQUEEN:
> Has an insidious ring to it, don't it?

JOHN JOHN:
> Applied anthropologists, mostly. Work with endangered cultures and the generally downtrodden, set up systems and programs with cheese at the far end and call it social adjustment.

CORBIE TWA:
> Must number in the millions. How come they haven't worked with me? I'm as hungry as the next mucker.

LUNKER:
> You must be burdened with racial success. Hello, everyone, I stepped into the line in time to catch the boy's last entry.

JOHN JOHN:
Backloading you now, Lunker. Welcome aboard.
LUNKER:
Caught a freefalling message from someone named Bound for Ur. Ladon's been shut down in Antarctica. Word is, the tech is being dismantled and packaged—
JOHN JOHN:
Packaged? For what, storage?
LUNKER:
The dismantling's in reverse order, John John. Doesn't sound like storage. In any case, Bound for Ur hand-offs the rumour that the Lady at Ladon negotiated a new site for her sky baby. The world denies, well, almost all the world...
CORBIE TWA:
The devil delivers indeed.
BOGQUEEN:
Two and two makes four. How the hell did the boy know?
LUNKER:
If he's reading between the NOAC lines, and knows the Swamp like he seems to, he might've done his own adding up. Four equals all hell busting loose.
CORBIE TWA:
This makes the boy hot, don't it.
BOGQUEEN:
Assuming NOAC reads his mail.
CORBIE TWA:
You must be kidding. NOAC reads everyone's mail. Readin it right now, in fact. Right fellas?
BOGQUEEN:
Comments, John John?...
CORBIE TWA:
Huh, he's slipped out.
STONECASTER:
Sorry I'm late. You guys and your random activations. Give

me a break next time, I'm antiquated and clunking macrotemporally. Give me a minute while I catch up.

LUNKER:

What's that buzz?

STONECASTER:

Shut up.

FREE WHIZZY:

What's needed here, muckers, is some encryption, and I'm your ticket-puncher. Rally my way and we'll plunge so deep NOAC will grope and grope and grope.

BOGQUEEN:

Double me up, Free Whizzy. I want John John to find us. Hey, didn't you get virused by NOAC last year?

FREE WHIZZY:

A worm in my brain. I had a transplant. They're still chasing me, or am I chasing them? Let's keep them guessing.

CORBIE TWA:

Two plus two, the Lady's made a deal. Oh my oh my oh my.

# Three

Entry: American N.W. 3 July, A.C. 14

The snow was just a memory. Overhead the sun burned away the clouds. On the ground the damp lichen curled its edges, mosses stiffened and crunched underfoot, and the ancient grey lichen strains formed snakeskin patterns on the boulders they would devour for the next hundred thousand years.

Three turkey vultures rode the thermals above the baking plain. Their feathers were glossy, flashing sunlight as they wheeled. At certain angles they disappeared entirely, as if plunging into a placid tropical sea, then re-emerged in sudden blooms of blinding light.

He watched them swing southward, seeking the heart of the Hole. Orders were orders. He'd set the beacon on the largest of the nearest tipi ring's weight stones. The beacon squatted like a turtle, silently chirping. The outside world homed in on its song, and he waited.

Hydrogen-fuelled, the helishuttle plunged earthward in a vapour mist of its own making. Down, down from the north, half its shielded face mirroring the raging sun. As it swept down, its delta wings infolded themselves into the craft's bright self. The blades hovered an amber circle above the machine's body, sharpened their declivity as podded feet touched earth.

William deactivated the beacon, walked to the crest of the hill, and watched four figures emerge from the helishuttle.

Tech Team, decked out in Cardinal Locator helmets, four black-lidded eyes facing in four directions to feed a 360 degrees comprehensive image back to the inside receiver. Wearing solar conductor butterfly blades rising up fourfold from their shoulder cowls. Multifunctioned, moisture grabbing, energy hoarding, rad and humidity sensing. Reflective insulated boots hiding their feet, cow-soled in shape and the colour of burnished brass.

CL helmets, lenses each set on separate array; motion detection to the right, seeing red on the left, human spectrum straight ahead and telephoto macro-capacities straight back.

Chest control pads, monitor feeds, glittering in the sunlight that moved, up and down, down and up their four selves. Static discharges marked friction points as the four figures walked forward.

Behind them the helishuttle squatted its round self on another hill, its four glider wings arched high to vent heat. The blades were now angled back and slowly rotating. The helishuttle's canopy had shifted shades, arriving at beryl. Its round self squatted, and above it was a roundness in kind, shaped by the rotating blades.

"I'm surprised you're still standing, William."

He blinked at the crimson expellation of her words, then looked beyond to the vague throne hovering behind her, suspended a dozen meters in the air. The other three activated their CLs and scanned for life and found what life they scanned and the living creatures found no place to hide.

"Is this your multiculture team, Dr. MacAlister?"

"Just the outriders, William. Listen, I'm thinking now we should bring you in, soon. You haven't been covering up, have you? Goddammit, William, at least activate your goggles."

"Soon. What do you need first?"

"The Lakota have fucked up, William. Something awful. You wouldn't believe the extent of the transgressions against pre-established agreements, especially the Covenants of '07. NOAC won't play nice-guy in this, William. I want you to tell Daniel

Horn. He's a little boy fucking with grown-ups, and he's going to get hurt, him and everyone behind him."

"Dr. MacAlister, there are layers to this rebellion. It has a long-standing precedent, wouldn't you say? We fuck them over, they fuck Custer over, we fuck them over, we fuck them over, we fuck them over—"

"William."

"And now they fuck us over. You keeping count, Dr. MacAlister? I think they're due."

"Don't let propaganda poison your scientific detachment, William. You need to stay rational about this. People could die, William."

"Am I to be scientifically detached, Doctor, or bound by guilt and threats? Can you really have both like that?"

"I don't care how you swallow it ethically, William. You deliver my message. We have to negotiate directly with Daniel Horn. Before the world mourns this tragedy, before you're left lamenting your weaknesses, before NOAC closes the book on the Lakota Nation."

She left food for his mouth, he showed her a flaked stone tool, bifacial perfection in the style called Eden. He set it against his forehead as they returned to their round machine with its round halo. He felt the blade cool against his brow, and knew it protected him for ten thousand years.

He knew adamant to be a fractious material, rife with flaws and phenocryst arbitrariness. An item of glittering admiration, but nothing he could work with. This wasn't adamant, this was chalcedony, and it was magic in a master's hands.

His kit was packed, supplies shouldered. He left the hill. He left the beacon where it sat like a turtle on the rock, ready to be discovered by a curious crow. He walked into the valley, forded the creek, ascended and descended a half dozen more hills, came to the closed road and walked down it, southward, until he found the barrier and the armed Lakota with their scarves and armbands and laser-tracking thunder-sticks.

He waited beyond the anti-assault mines, hunkered down on the cracked blacktop, and studied a corkscrew cactus with shiny flat spines that rotated away from the sun with perfect precision as the hours passed. Tiny white spiders spun webs between the spines, created balls of liquid that turned sticky and mimed droplets of condensation. The spiders clung to the underside of the spines, and waited.

A skimmer arrived and landed behind the barricade. Daniel Horn passed through the shock line and carefully made his way to William.

"Mother wants to talk."

Daniel shrugged. "I'll think about it. I'm worried as hell about you, William. Those conjuctiva are there to tell you something. Something important."

"I see beyond them, Daniel."

"Fuck, you can barely blink. Here, use my goggles; they're the best you can buy."

"No. Mother's spirit is in me. She tastes bitter."

"We're naughty boys, are we?"

"Impudent and stiffhearted. Threats were made. People could die."

"They want a ball of fire, they'll get it. The oil fields are rigged, and I mean subsurface rigged. The earth will melt, William. They can kill us, but they'll get nothing for it, nothing left to plunder. We'll butcher the buffalo, William, all of them. Call it manifest destiny; that's something they'll understand."

"I've disappeared, Daniel. My days as a messenger are over. Tell her yourself."

"Still making your entries on the Net?"

"Like droplets of condensation."

"That'll do."

"It will?"

Daniel's smile was a broken effort. "If you're the boy and I think you are. Please, William, pull yourself out."

"I can't. I must speak of my captivity, Daniel. I must explore its absence. And all the ghosts are walking with me now. They're an insistent bunch, Daniel."

"Hell, William."

"I found a paleo-point. Eden style. Ten thousand years old. Knife River flint. Here, it's yours. At least in its physical manifestation. I imagine you can see the imprint on my forehead. That's its ghost, thus I am marked, and thus it shall be. Like that spear head of old, I am hunting big game. The biggest."

## NOAC NET:

...announcement today confirms the rumour that Ladon Incorporated and the Lakota Nation have reached an agreement that in the words of NOAC Spokesperson Dr. Jenine MacAlister, "represents the most serious threat in terms both economic and political."

This follows fierce debate and accusations in the New United Nations assembly, presently in an extraordinary session following the near-collapse of all world markets. Saudi Arabia was accused by both NOAC and SINJO of failing to comply with the trade embargo against the Ladon Corporation, which was enacted exactly three years ago today (July 4, A.C. 11). Spokespersons for the Saudi contingent have responded that a legal loophole was exploited by Ladon regarding the retrieval of Ladon technology from Saudi territory; a legalistic sleight of hand similar to the one employed against Argentina at Boxwell Plateau, Antarctica.

The NUN world court, which Ladon refuses to recognise, is now considering immediate corrective measures to close this loophole, anticipating copy-cat pressures from other free corporations to avoid contractual obligations to their parent nations.

Indeed, two small corporations with contract and material ties to Ladon have reportedly 'abandoned' high technology on unpatrolled shoals off the African Coast which was subsequently salvaged under Charter 70109 of the NUN Salvage Rights, by Ladon Corporation.

This flagrant circumvention of the NUN...

...NOAC Security has announced an intensive program to clean up the Net's infamous 'swamp,' after an encrypted exchange of unknown information was briefly tracked by Security monitors...

...Normal pursuit measures encountered an heretofore unknown tracksweeper with hidden mines, resulting in loss of trail and minor damage to the Security Insystem.

"This constitutes a premeditated evasion of information by parties unknown, contrary to the NUN Charters defining universal access to information on the Net." The release goes on to say that a list of suspects has been compiled and is being pursued "with rancour."

...Pakistani forces retreat in face of Sikh incursions and once again yield the Khyber Pass...

..."Hidden" stock market remains a likely candidate for culpability in latest market crash...

...NOAC Economic Security officials "closer to Ladon's list of secret shareholders."

...Boreal Forest joins the list of Near Extinct ecosystems. But as Forestry Spokesman Arnold Sheer noted, "The Boreal forest is notoriously low in energy yield. The bio-spheres are virtually inconsequential in global yield terms." The designation for the Boreal Forest now adds this ecosystem to coral reefs, tropical and temperate rain forests and tundra. As has been noted, however, the deforested areas are now viable for agricorp expansions...

...the new virus infecting the East Codfarms has necessitated destroying over four thousand tonnes of fish stock. Economic and resource projections suggest a new designation to Red-3 level for Dependent Peoples. Given the trans-species characteristic of this new virus, the slaughtered fish could not be used as Feed for domesticates. The East Codfarms was the last marine farm still operating. Open Seas monitoring indicates little change in the now empty oceans world-wide. The official statement goes on to emphasise that there is no cause for panic, as GMO and GrowVat Foodstocks remain at optimum levels...

...four months into the excavation, with complete capping of the site set to begin immediately. The Mars Palaeontology Team is now officially dissolved following an undisclosed breach of security...

...SINJI re-affirms military aid ties with India, at a historic meeting of officials outside Tel-abib on the banks of the Chebar River, where they arose and went forth into the plain and there spoke with each other and no-one else, for this was a plain of darkness where he sang nevermore RECALL? SYSTEM ERROR SINJI SOURCE RECALL in all damnation, for they are rebellious in their houses...

SFI 29786.17
Subject: Site Mj-eb 21
Subcategory: Mars Excavation Projects
Abstract: Sediments firmly dated at 11.2-13.3 mya yield gracile hominid fossil remains and evidence of an extensive agricultural complex in the XXXXXXX region of the Santo Regina basin—

Tracking...
Captured.
NF NF NF

Entry: American N.W. 4 July, A.C. 14

In her blind world, she lay under the rock and listened. Burned blind, but eyes had become irrelevant. She thought nothing of this. Painless, forgotten. At night she would slide out from her place of rest, threading through the grasses and bouncing echoes off the land around her. Hunting, and there was food for her mouth in plenty. The rodents were everywhere, for a time unrestrained in their nightly activities. But she'd adapted, more or less overnight, along with a good many of her sisters. Granted, some took another route. No problem there. In any case, the snake was in heaven.

Beneath the rock, her newly sensitised ears detected the presence of humans. She felt probing sonar bounce off the rock she lay under, and other probes as well, but her blood was cold, and they found her not.

"I haven't really got the time for this, Dr. MacAlister."

"The Lady's put you in charge of the project. You bastard, what the hell do you think you're doing?"

"What?"

"Is my language excessive, Max? Come on, give me a fucking break. These Lakota are dependent on us. If they cut NOAC out, they cut their own throat."

"Take it up with them, Doctor. I've got an engineering problem to tackle. Being intercepted has messed up my schedule."

"You passed through NOAC airspace, Max. Hell, I could've ordered you shot down."

"Why didn't you? It's the only way you can stop us."

"I want some messages delivered. Both ways."

"And those messages are?"

"For the Lakota. The embargo is officially NUN approved. Extreme sanctions. Assets seized, the works. Nothing goes in, nothing comes out."

"I can hear Horn already. Back to the reservations, right?"

"You're missing the point. Tell the Lady this, Max. You may have made a deal with the Lakota Nation, but the Lakota Nation is finished. No money for you—I don't think the Lady will swing this one past her secret shareholders. Ladon will be financially ruined."

"No money was involved, Dr. MacAlister. Basic reciprocity in action. The Lakota appreciated the irony, by the way. After all, it's the way they used to do things, isn't it?"

"I'm not done with my message to Ladon. No air corridors will be granted. Your supplies will never reach here. Any efforts to breach the free-air zone will be met militarily."

"Anything else?"

"Deliver the messages, Max. The world doesn't want your project to get off the ground. Period. It's dangerous, untested—"

"Right, the official line. Come on, Doctor, we both know why NOAC and SINJO, and EUROCOM for that matter, are pissing themselves. It's economic, pure and simple. Or, rather, if you'll excuse my blunt language, bloody greed. Ladon's not offering a piece of the pie, and you're all offended. Stopping us is your obsession, Jenine. You and your bosses. The Lady has a message for you, all of you, and it's this: stop panicking, you might get your piece of the pie, eventually. But only if you're nice."

"You're exploiting the Lakota—"

"Bullshit. They aren't children, Doctor. Never were, despite your most cherished beliefs. The noble savage was your creation, Doctor, not theirs. They won't live in a bottle of your making. Hell, you want to see the effects of your social engineering programs, look in your own backyard. God never granted you the right to fuck around with other people's cultures."

"Who's speaking?"

"A snake whispering in your ear, Doctor. She's bored under that rock, waiting for night. She echo-located you out of the ether. You were just passing by, but her hunting instincts are up, and she's with you now, with her newly reflective skin that makes her invisible, a ghost at your ear, whispering."

"I've been placed in an untenable position."

"And it's all yours, Jenine."

"Go to hell."

"I'm already here."

---

NET:

LUNKER:
    Another streamer from Bound for Ur, friends. This stuff must come from an Inner Ear, if you catch my drift.

VORPAL:
    I can't believe what I'm reading. NOAC's got spy sats tracking every Ladon shipment on the whole goddamn planet?

LUNKER:
    Desperate measures... I admit my back's up on this. Look, we've all been chased before, so we know how it feels.

BLANC KNIGHT:
    The Lady's not human, friends. She's something else entirely. Something more than human.

LUNKER:
    You anticipating she's going to drop a perfumed scarf, Blanco?

BLANC KNIGHT:
    I'll take it up if she does, Lunker.

VORPAL:
    Bravo, sirrah! Count me in.

LUNKER:
> If the Lady's as uncanny as you say, she isn't likely the kind to ask for help. I'd think she can manage her own battles. She's done it so far.

VORPAL:
> Things aren't looking good right now, though. At least that's what between the lines from Bound for Ur.

BLANC KNIGHT:
> Well, we're looking at spy sats, correct? I mean, they're rather small and delicate, aren't they? Microsats usually are.

VORPAL:
> Indeed, and of course com sats are much larger. We'd need to loop in and get a tracking matrix on the eye-spies—

BLANC KNIGHT:
> Not necessary. Bound for Ur's provided us with transport routes for all of Ladon's shipments. We've got times, dates, lats and longs. The eye-spies will be right on them. Ergo.

VORPAL:
> I'm setting up for a com sat interface now. Where's my Nintendo joystick? You with me on this, Blanco?

BLANC KNIGHT:
> Let me know which one you grab, and I'll feed you the co-ords on the nearest eye-spy.

VORPAL:
> Lovely.

LUNKER:
> You guys are scary. Hey, anybody skimming the official news lately? Some weird things going on.

. . .

LUNKER:
> Hello?

NET:

JOHN JOHN:
NOACom:
> THIS IS AN UNRESTRICTED LINE. GO BACK. YOU ARE NOT CLEARED FOR THIS LINE.

JOHN JOHN:
NOACom:
> FREEDOM FILES REQUIRE CLEARANCE. WHO IS THIS, PLEASE?

JOHN JOHN:
NOACom:
> Freedom Files: In keeping with the NUN Charters and Conventions, all information is accessible to all citizens. Freedom Files represents a block of accessible information assembled by NOAC, SINJO, EUROCOM and other National Cartels. This information block complies with all NUN Charters and Conventions. This information is an unrestricted line, and is accessible to all citizens.

JOHN JOHN:
NOACom:
> YOU ARE NOT CLEARED TO ACCESS FREEDOM FILES, CITIZEN. GO BACK, OR PROSECUTION AS UNOFFICIAL USAGE WILL RESULT. WARNING, PROHIB FUNCTIONS ON THIS LINE WILL DESTROY YOUR SYSTEM AS A PUNITIVE MEASURE. IDENTITY WILL BE DETERMINED AND ALL ASSETS SEIZED. GO BACK.

JOHN JOHN:
NOACom:
> YEAH WELL FUCK YOU, TOO>.

## Lakota Nation, Terminal Zone, 5 July, A.C. 14

The small tracked machine circled him from a distance at first, then began spiralling closer. After a while, he stopped walking and waited for it.

Its four sensor eyes examined him in turn, the metallic half-dome swivelling with a faint hum. Its steel chest opened up to reveal a monitor screen. The image flickered, then steadied to reveal Jenine McAlister's face.

Her voice came from a speaker above the monitor. "So one of my searchers found you. Good. Please speak clearly when you record. I assume you have delivered the appeal to Daniel Horn. What was the answer? Will they talk?"

William glanced up to see a hooded hawk circling overhead. Earlier, he'd panicked a score of shiny mice on a knoll. They had been collectively weaving blades of grass, making long green tunnels between den holes. The mice seemed to possess extra digits on their front paws. William couldn't be certain—the mice quickly disappeared down their holes—but the weave of the grass blades looked intricate, precise.

A new voice came from the speaker: "The recording device is voice activated. Please speak to activate the recording device."

A loud roar startled William. He looked back into the sky to see the hawk diving earthward. Far above, like a piece of the sun, a ball of white fire descended. Amber smoke poured from it in a tail. It cut its way across the sky, spinning, flinging burning fragments out to the sides. The roaring sound deepened.

William raised a hand to cover his eyes. His attention was drawn to the skin of his hand. Burned, blistered, the first epidermal layers cracked and yellowing. His fingerprints were gone.

A distant detonation to the southwest. Thunder beneath his feet, then silence.

He closed his broken lips on the spitter, drew in a mouthful of recycled water. A taste like ashes. He blinked rapidly, but the blank spots continued to swim across his vision. Blank, like patches of snow on a grey day.

He saw the helishuttles before he heard them. They flew in formation, miming the contours of the ground; skimming hilltops, plunging down into valleys. They approached quickly, on a route that would take them nearly over his head. The muffled sound of their blades barely carried on the wind.

William stared, blinking and shifting his head as they swept into and out of blind spots. A moment later the helishuttles reared up in front of him, then over. He saw the Ladon logo on their underbellies, a dragon coiled around a tree against a black field. He swung round and continued staring after them.

"The recording device is voice activated. Please speak to activate the recording device. Camera is recording."

William tried to smile, but his lips split and he winced. He opened his mouth and crouched down to one of the visual sensors. He stuck out his swollen tongue, tried to move it, then withdrew it, closed his bleeding mouth and sat back, shrugging.

He looked down at his hands, closed them into fists. His skin and flesh felt waxy. He dug his nails into his palms. As good as a candlestick, and this monitor, on this machine programmed to return to her, is as good as a plaster wall. So I come forth, the fingers of a man's hand, and so that you may see the part of the hand that wrote, here on this shiny screen.

William reached out to the screen, then hesitated. Someone crouched down beside him. William glanced over, nodded. I recall the photograph, the days at the fort, during that hard winter. You weren't wearing rad goggles back then, of course. But you've been disarmed a thousand times, old man, haven't you.

Sitting Bull shrugged, then grasped William's hand. I will guide you thereon, in this message. I will write this for you.

Who will read it?

She cannot. Daniel can, but she will never ask him. All the records have been sealed, and this language of pictures, ancient as it is, is nevertheless complicated, for our thoughts were never simple.

Of course they weren't.

Do you know, the ghosts are dancing?

Is that your message?

Clever boy. We've known that all along, your cleverness. Even so, this spirit you quest for, it changes our countenance and leads us into doubt.

I make no grand claims, Sitting Bull.

This spirit you quest for, it is your own?

I'm not sure. I still keep denying it.

Sitting Bull finished guiding his hand, and let it fall. He smiled at William. Blindness inside and out. Here, take my goggles.

No, thanks.

Tell me, William Potts, will your final fire be hot?

Hot as hell. Don't say I didn't warn you.

The machine swivelled its eyes one last time, then crawled away, northward. William rose and retrieved his backpack. Far to the southwest pillars of smoke reached skyward in a row, each pulled to one side by the steady wind. William squinted. Four, maybe five pillars. It was getting hard to tell things like that.

Sitting Bull was gone, but that was something he'd always known.

---

Jim's Story:

Saskatchewan, Canada, 30th June, A.D. 2004

Jim had stopped asking why he was still here. The question had run through his mind again and again, until it seemed to fall into the rhythm of his heart, his breathing, each swing of the shovel, each toss of the bale. But now he'd stopped, like a clock running down into silence, down into a world without time.

Chubb, the red heeler, came into view from around the barn, prowling, nose testing the air for any new scent of cat. Jim wasn't sure, but he figured that there was at least one left, hiding somewhere. Hell of a mean dog. Mean mean mean. Still, haven't got the heart to put him under. The Morrisons lost the ranch so fast, and now the old beater's got no cows to chase. Besides, cats don't kick back. Hell, though, I liked all the cats. Reminded me of Ruth, of course, and Albert, and the way things used to be.

It was in his head now, the old voice in his blood rising like a chant. The land had never been kind, but it had become downright vicious lately. He'd done his best to turn things over. Farming had sucked the land dry and dead, and without Ruth's school-learning in the finer points of modern agriculture, the profits had quickly vanished. He'd tried to turn the land back, back to its original state. Pasture, cattle, the prairie regained from the exhausted, topsoil-stripped earth, the combines rusting into motionless hulks in beds of high grass. But it had been way too late, and righting the wrong tasted sour, for one simple reason: he was the only one left.

Grandpa dead of a heart attack, Ruth dead of ovarian cancer, Albert dead three days after his second birthday to leukaemia.

The night past had seen a wind storm, a real duster—walls of black airborne dirt trudging across the hills—no rain, just wind, scouring the paint from the barn's west wall, pitting the house's siding, chewing leaves from the branches of the trees in the windbreak. He'd woken this morning to an ochre sky with the sun a mere blush of pink. And his backyard had changed—ten inches of soil stripped away, right down to the gravel that had been left behind by glaciers ten thousand years past, and on this lumpy bed of limestone cobbles curled-up skeletons lay in clumps. Scores of them. The wind had exposed a burial ground, right there in his goddamned back yard.

Jim lit a cigarette to get the taste of dust out of his mouth. He watched Chubb pause at the front wheel of one of the university trucks, lift a leg and give it a wet what-for. A bunch of scientists were crawling round among the bones out back. The head archaeologist had told Jim that there'd been a blow-out site just like this one about ninety minutes northwest of here, years back, called the Gray Site. It'd been right beside a farmhouse, too, one that had seen more bankruptcies and more owners than any other in the area. Jim grunted, not surprised.

The burial ground was an old one, from way before the time of the Cree, Assiniboine and Lakota. Four thousand years old, before horses, which explained why there were as many dogs buried there as people. The archaeologist had shown him a dog's vertebra, the way the edges had compacted from a lifetime of pulling travois. Down the slope aways was a larger jumble of bones: women and children. The damned dogs got more ceremony than did the women and children.

Bloody scientists, the second bunch this month. The other group had come to test his well water. Statistically high incidences of cancers in the area. Someone's thesis in biochemistry. The well was foul, but Jim had known that all along. Herbicidal residue, pesticides, lead, mercury. And maybe an angry water spirit, loose somewhere down below, unappeased and full of venom.

It was no wonder that Chubb seemed so at home here. No wonder at all. Mean dog, mean, mean. Mean.

There was going to be trouble. That citified Indian from Winnipeg, Jack Tree, had been stirring things up with pushing land claims back into the Supreme Court. News of the burial ground was bound to feed his fires, even though the people buried were from so long ago that their closest relatives probably lived somewhere in Mexico. Or so the archaeologist said. Jack Tree would know that, and he wouldn't give a damn. He'd play on public ignorance, he'd raise a wave of emotion and ride it as far as he could.

It's not right. I got more ties to this damn land than Jack Tree. He's from South Dakota, for Christ's sake. He thinks he can sit behind a mike in Ottawa and take it all away from me. The hell with that.

Bloody hot summer, too. The hottest yet.

The cat bolted into view, a tawny shot from under his pickup. Chubb ducked his head, muscles rippling as he raced in explosive pursuit.

Jim sighed. He'd liked all the cats.

## NET:

**FREE WHIZZY:**
Everybody still with me?
**BOGQUEEN:**
Murky world here. Devonian.
**CORBIE TWA:**
Antediluvian.
**FREE WHIZZY:**
So the boy's name is William, and he's got friends in high places.
**BOGQUEEN:**
I'm not sure that was a friendly contact.
**STONECASTER:**
No reason to think it wasn't, Bogqueen. Sure, maybe they argued a bit, but how much of that was for our benefit? Think about it. We've got some guy named William walking around under the Midwest Hole. He's inputting on a field notebook, but somehow he's hack enough to slice through every Security Block and swim the Swamp. Nobody catches him, nobody intercepts, nobody shuts him down. I admit it, I've got some serious doubts about all this.
**CORBIE TWA:**
You're slagging NOAC with a whole lot of heavy cunning, Stonecaster. Come on, these politicos aren't that subtle.
**STONECASTER:**
Really. Psychotic geniuses are a dime a dozen in any security arm of any gov't you'd care to mention. Diabolical's the word, I kid you not.

BOGQUEEN:
> Unsupported conclusions, Stonecaster. Look at the info he's dropping our way. The contraventions are serious stuff. Straight from that historical cesspool NOAC and co. keep telling us is unimportant, outdated. But if you try getting close, for a better look at that cesspool, they cook your computer, grab your assets, and the next thing you know they've busted down the door and you're penal-tagged. Sweeping streets for the rest of your miserable life.

FREE WHIZZY:
> What kind of contraventions, Bogqueen? I think you've lost most of us. So far, the boy's mentioned a handful of creepy-crawlies that seem to have adapted to high rad no-ozone toxic environments. This is blasphemy?

BOGQUEEN:
> Keep up on the literature? Anyone? There's a party line on this stuff, the university and ministry backed monographs are pushing a revised world view that justifies gov't policy. It's there in the science, in the reams of squirreled data they keep publishing.

STONECASTER:
> Cure for insomnia.

BOGQUEEN:
> Precisely. They don't want you to actually analyse the data, or the parameters of the study. Skip to the conclusions. And the manufactured Zeitgeist builds momentum, quietly, invasively and insidiously.

FREE WHIZZY:
> Elucidate us, Bogqueen.

BOGQUEEN:
> It's a kind of twisted systems theory. A few decades ago the industrial age ran up against environmental mysticism, and the shit started flying. People started noticing—or maybe finally listening to people who'd been screaming their terror for years—anyway, the subjects of mass extinction came up

repeatedly. Deforestation, destruction of habitats, and species extinction rates climbing exponentially. Add that to increased rates of human toxemia, resistant diseases, herbicide and pesticide overkill, rad leaks at reactor plants, not to mention terrorists flicking Biks and you've got people running for the wilderness and the Great Mother who's real sick and needs mending. You've got militants ready to kill to defend the lowland gorilla, and fuck the Chinese healers with their mortars and pestles and their demands for more gorilla hands, bear livers, whatever. Anyway, the industrial revolution started losing momentum—especially with increased mechanisation and skyrocketing unemployment. Compassion for the world and its nonhuman inhabitants grew, became a political force it wasn't safe to ignore anymore. Through all this, the academic community poured out supporting data for the environmentalists. They were allies, and they made a helluva team in a world confused enough to depend almost entirely on experts and specialists.

CORBIE TWA:
So the gov't got clever. Rest your vocal chords, Bogqueen, I'll run a ways with the story. You others still with us?

STONECASTER:
Waiting to see you pin the tail on the donkey. I figure you're somewhere between Jupiter and Mars.

FREE WHIZZY:
I'm listening.

PACEMAKER:
I've been listening all along, but I figured I'd show myself, what the hell. Surfing your wave down here wasn't easy, so I'm feeling pretty good about myself right now. How forward of me.

BOGQUEEN:
Hi. No sign of John John?

STONECASTER:
'Fraid not. Maybe he got nabbed.

CORBIE TWA:
> Back to the story, then. The Net was on line by then, or at least a version of it. The world started talking, and it started getting hard for gov'ts to keep their citizens sufficiently myopic. Info bled everywhere. Security parameters were a joke. Ideas had arrived, and once voiced there was no turning back. Pop goes the cork. So the gov'ts got clever, like I said. Flood the lines with useless information and call it unrestricted access. Meanwhile, pull the funding chain on the universities and call it enlightened merger. Faculties became Ministries, the cynical academics suddenly found themselves in charge of social policy, students became gov't trainees, and mandatory university enrolment was the funnel. Out the other end, an endless spewing forth of ideas, carefully shaped opinions and general consensus. Combine that with full employment and a penal system that put the countless criminals and malcontents to blue-collar work, and you've got a prosperous, paranoid but happy populace. The Jihad stuff fit perfectly, giving the gov'ts all the power they wanted. Things were good for them right about then. Except for all the wars and the Big Crash that took down the old US of A. And the Mideast debacle and all those nukes being thrown around—

BOGQUEEN:
> You're digressing, Corbie. To focus all that, one of the big ideas that took hold unplugged the environmental movement. First, you had the alliance fucked up. People with power quickly quit complaining or making dire predictions. Second, and this was the idea itself, concocted by the academics in dry tones: life is characterised by periods of mass extinction. We may have accelerated this one, but that's all just relative. What you're seeing is an inevitable expression of Nature. The Great Mother wipes clean the slate, once again. Relax everyone. Can't fight the inevitable and, really, should you? Natural order is natural order, after all. Go with the

flow, sure it's sad, but it's better feeling sad than feeling guilt-ridden.

**CORBIE TWA:**
Naturally, we bought it, with a world-wide sigh of relief. Absolved at last, pass the salt.

**BOGQUEEN:**
Ozone depletion, oh well, it was bound to happen eventually. We've adapted, with our rad shielding and unguents and elixirs. No different from all those volcanic eruptions on the Rim. Too bad about those rad leaks in Asia, and as for those peripheral human populations, we can help them.

**CORBIE TWA:**
Help indeed. That's what the boy's gnawing at, isn't it.

**STONECASTER:**
But he's one of those students you were talking about. Why isn't he converted?

**PACEMAKER:**
He was probably too sharp for his own good. And given his talent on the Net, he might well have accessed the so-called unrestricted files, which contain, among other things, a whole list of forbidden subjects, repressed data analyses, heretical theses, not to mention anthropological monographs, from which one can cull the most surprising information. Historical revisionism is the official line, as you said. The forces of evolution can well serve deterministic notions, if misapplied. Even more disturbing, it can be philosophically extended to justify any means, given the inevitable end.

**BOGQUEEN:**
It's the extinction stuff that's now in trouble. William's out there recording field observations that run contrary to the mass extinction idea. The beasts are changing, because they're pressured populations. Out there we're getting leap-frog speciation, at a phenomenal rate of mutation.

**PACEMAKER:**
There are profound implications to that notion.

BOGQUEEN:
> You'd better effing well believe it. And there is a political side to that last entry. Never mind the telepathic snake, that conversation between Dr. Jenine MacAlister and Max Ohman provided a pretty succinct statement of the issues.

FREE WHIZZY:
> Who's Max Ohman?

BOGQUEEN:
> The Lady's right hand boy. Ladon's Chief Engineer.

FREE WHIZZY:
> Well, I can see how the theoretical stuff might trigger some kind of philosophical ruckus, but I still can't grasp the risk to the politicos.

BOGQUEEN:
> It's too soon to tell, really. I'd rather not speculate. Besides, I've got faith in the boy.

STONECASTER:
> You must be crazy. The kid's cooked. If he's not pulled out, he'll be dead inside a week.

BOGQUEEN:
> I know. He's running out of time.

CORBIE TWA:
> Maybe that's his real message.

...

---

NET:

... Behold, I am the back door, and my name is Malachai ...

JOHN JOHN:
> Who?

...

JOHN JOHN:

NOAC CENTRAL:
> This path is unauthorised. Contact NOAC through the means described in the NOAC Directory. This path is unauthorised.

JOHN JOHN:
> *******

NOAC CENTRAL:
> DISJUNCTIVE ACCESS, File opening now...

Directory:
> NOAC CENTRAL\MINISTRY OF SOCIAL EQUALIZATION\USASK COMPLX Path: DATA ACQUISITION\ANALYSIS, DEPT APPLIED ANTHRO\MCALISTER, J...
>> Contents:
>>> PERSONNEL
>>> POPULATIONS
>>> PROJECTS
>>> PROJECTIONS
>>> XTND BIO ANLYSES

JOHN JOHN:
> **********

USASK:
> Contents:
>> NOAC
>>> * BRAZIL
>>> * PACIFIC S.& C. AMERICA
>>> * ATLANTIC/CARIB S.& C. AMERICA
>>> * HOPI CONFED (pre-mass suicide)
>>> * LAKOTA NATION
>>> * WEST CST NATION
>>> * CENTRAL INUIT CONFED
>>> * UNSETTLED NOAC POPULATIONS
>> SINJO
>>> * CENTRL ASIA
>>> * N.E. COAST

EUROCOM
    * GYPSIES
    * LAPLANDER CONFED
OTHERS
    * AFRICAN TRIBAL
    * PACIFIC ISLES
    * AUSTRAL/ZEALAND/GUINEA

JOHN JOHN:

    *******\********* ******

USASK:

GENETIC ANALYSIS subsection only file presently ported.

JOHN JOHN:

    ****** ********

USASK:

Date of last entry: APRIL 09/2012 GENETIC ANALYSIS of PERIPHERAL POPULATION OVERGROUP FINNOSLAVIC, LAPLANDER (see synonyms cat6B) DETERMINED SECOND GENERATION ADAPTIVE TRAITS:

(field and sample observer: GBM)

    * Radiation resistivity:

-semipermeable membrane detected on liver of subject; biopsy analysis incomplete but suggests new function based on mutated cell walls and armored nuclei (cf. file cytology 23), the latter previously observed at other non-regenerative areas.

    * Homeostatic Mechanisms:

Overall reduction in body mass: with increased ratio of mass to surface; Increased fluid retention (without accompanying loss of body heat) and increased functionality of retained fluid;

    * UV Shield & Defence Mechanisms:

> Multilayered retinas with nascent regenerative capacities; epicanthic folds around eyes; altered sleep cycle; melanin detected in lenses; reflective body-hair (follicle is flat and edged, with high oil content)
>
> * Resistance to Toxins:
>> Overall flushing mechanisms as indicated by flush glands that concentrate toxins then expurgate through bowel tract (glands still incomplete);
>
> * Nonspecified adaptations:
>> Expanded visual spectrum to include marginal infrared detection; other traits common to all pressured populations (see notes)

NOAC:
> INTERCEPT

JOHN JOHN:

USASK:
> Return to previous menu?

NOAC:
> INTERCEPT & TRACKING

JOHN JOHN:
> Shit.

NOAC:
> TRACKING

JOHN JOHN:

NOAC:
> TRACKING

JOHN JOHN:

NOAC:
> CAPTURED

USASK:
> Security Class 7 you are UNAUTHORISED to proceed further.

NOAC:
    Where am I?
USASK:
    NOAC Security File, Shunt 2761B, Personnel, Codename Hackhunter.
NOAC:
    That's me, you assholes.
USASK:
    Subject of file is UNAUTHORISED to access contents.
NOAC:
    What the fuck. You pricks, I'm one of the good guys.
USASK:
    Subject of file is UNAUTHORISED to access contents. GO BACK.
NOAC:
    Shunt this to Securicom. Pissing off the good guys is bad business. Hackhunter signing off. For good.

# Four

American N.W. Terminal Zone, 7 July, A.C. 14

A year for every day.
Decay of plastic welds. His bootsuit was falling apart beneath the invisible torrent from the cloudless sky. Earlier, at dawn, he'd woken in his shield tent to the roar of machinery. Climbing out, he saw a thousand combines cresting a nearby ridge, emerging from a storm of dust and toppling mindlessly over the steep embankment. Loping along the ridge, almost invisible in their reflective fur, a half dozen coyotes appeared, observing their handiwork. He listened to them laugh.

And the sun rose once again.

He sipped thick, acidic water from the spitter, then slowly lowered his backpack. Now noon, the place he had found himself in was a dead-ground. Leaning barns, silos with peeling walls, dead oak trees and a farmhouse encircled by abandoned machinery. A last circling of the wagons, but it had been useless. The red skins were in the mirror.

No ghosts here, simply the thunderous silence of their absence. William looked around, blinking painfully as he studied the detritus of his own kind, and smelled the poison in the air. Subsurface leakage, coming up from the well near the barn.

Pesticides, herbicides, concentrations in the water table like lifeless jellyfish.

A strange, almost incandescent moss covered the cinder-blocks lining the well, had spread outward to cover three plastic leprechauns with an oily, vaguely translucent patina. Two plaster fawns crouched in the skeletal shade of the dead oaks, their paint faded, but still the animals stood, frozen immobile by terror. In their eyes, nothing but white.

William almost laughed. Zombie bambis, hallelujah. He wished he could laugh. He hadn't laughed in so long.

Dehydration. Mustn't run out of moisture.

He walked over to the well, set his blistered hands on the cool moss covering the cinder-blocks, leaned over and looked down. A pool, viscid in shades of blue, magenta, bottlefly green. Pale round waterbugs swam dizzying circles beneath the surface. Damn things didn't even need air anymore. William straightened and took a few steps backward.

He removed a flare from his belt, activated it and tossed it into the well.

Fire! A pillar of poisonous flame! He watched it eating a vertical path skyward. A sudden eye glares upward, and meets the steady polished eye of a satellite. They study each other, then wink with their own designs.

I anoint this dead-ground, absolution of its sins burning into oblivion, whilst the scarabs beneath the surface of a dead skin race down into cool darkness, and there await the coming of their first breaths. Savage oxygen, the lungs that birth the cough of flame.

I see you all come closer, drawn by this crisp cut to the air, this clean crackle which my dying hands have cast into the well of darkness.

Gather, then, while I bathe. When I emerge, you will be able to touch me, and I will be able to touch you. Our spirits will join, and we will march like a sea that swallows the earth. We will march, and none may stop us. Ghosts, we are all ghosts now. We must deliver the new world unto the inheritors, who know us not.

The dead-grounds are alive once again.

Behold this self, Daniel. I am Mene before the feast.

The water was like ice against his skin, as close to pain as he could remember. He carefully reattached the clasps on the rotting bootsuit, and scanned the ruined farm with new eyes.

The farm's battered arrogance had fallen in upon itself, and now the air was filled with ghosts, the streaming dead still mute but brimming with their separate stories. All eyes rested on him.

He would be their language, their words, now. He understood that much. He would speak for them all. God had given him the lie, laid bare and bleeding. We have lived in our heaven, and we have made it as it is. Somewhere above, the fallen angels still climb.

William stared at his hands. His sight had changed. The bones stood out sharply, solid in a fading haze of mortal flesh. Blood pulsed through the capillaries, faintly glowing.

He retrieved his backpack and stiffly worked his way into the straps. The pillar of fire had been sighted. Satellites, high altitude reconnaissance craft. Activity in the Hole. Pinpoint resolution, down to the water trickling from his hair. As attentively as these ghosts, machines watched him, recorded his movements, then dutifully reported the data. Still, the heat sensor records would baffle the analysers. Around him flowed an ice age, there in the breath of beasts dead for ten thousand years. They are my body, Daniel, and I am their voice.

His joints protested dully as he lurched into motion. Knees refusing to bend, balance awry, tottering and jolting forward, stalking like a stiff marionette.

The ghosts closed in, flowing and brushing against him, bolstering him upright with their gelid shoulders, broad wintry backs. Nearby, he saw a coyote and recognised it.

"I remember you. The last hunt. Bison antiquus. I see you keeping your distance, friend." The words were in his head, but so was everything else. No borders left, his skull porous, his thoughts drifting in the air, delicately traced by the satellites, and heard by the coyote.

"You're too old," William said, "for mere trickery. You were here and you were there, on the edge of that continental bridge. You watched our arrival. Did you know what it meant? Did you know then what it always means, friend?"

But the earth yields to the shovel, and is turned over, flipped onto its back. Again and again, this is what we do, and each time, the firmament fills with spirits departing the old ways. We move on. We never look back.

The coyote dropped back, then behind, into his wake. Ready to pick at the pieces, prepared as ever to contemplate the scatter of garbage, the meanings of the twisted tin can and the candy wrapper, the crushed velvet of moss beneath a tire's track. The coyote contemplates, and might even smile as the can rusts and withers to dust, as the wrapper crumbles under the sun, as the moss slowly springs back.

The coyote stays in our wake, and patiently awaits the coming of our bones, scattered like a sprung bundle of sticks. A disarticulated map to mull over, the wind moaning through the holes in our skull. It listens to that song, but soon tires of the repetition. In a world where nothing changes, we'd best move on.

Humped-back transports crawled a ritual dance on the plain below. William leaned sideways into the wind, his broken boots precariously gripping the edge of a ridge, and studied the mechanical dance on the valley floor. A score of smaller vehicles buzzed randomly through the greater design. He watched two converge, then drive out from the swarm, approaching him side-by-side, lumbering steadily up the slope.

Daniel and Jack Tree emerged from the vehicle on the left. A squat, wide man stepped out from the vehicle on the right. The stranger wore sunglasses and a baseball cap with the Ladon crest above the brim. His face was lined, clean-shaven, and almost flat, the bones underneath Mongoloid, the incisors in his maxilla and mandible shovel-shaped. A hairline crack along his zygoma revealed an old, poorly healed broken cheekbone.

"Can you hear me?" Daniel asked, stepping close.

William nodded.

"Can you see me?"

He nodded again. Cranial characteristics displayed the wondrous lineage of Daniel, so close to that of the Asian stranger. William turned and studied Jack Tree. Caucasoid traits for the most part. Even the bones contributed to the mask that had dissipated like smoke the possibilities of prejudice, a trick of sympathy that swayed the media, enraptured the public.

"See any spy teams out there, William?"

He looked back at Daniel.

"Sorry, applied anthropologists, then."

William shook his head.

"Our arrays picked up a heat signature," the stranger said, his wide-boned hands on his hips. "Big one. We tracked you from it."

William smiled, and said, "I would speak, if you can hear me."

The stranger frowned at Daniel, then shrugged. "I hear you fine, son."

"A pillar of flame. I am reborn to the hour. Watch me burn, gentlemen."

Jack Tree barked an uneasy laugh. "You're talking to an engineer, Potts, not some goddamned mystic."

"The fire is only the beginning," William said, steadying his gaze on Jack Tree, who stepped back. "The wheel will spin, and lightning will scar the sky. There'll be thunder, but from the earth. And the clouds will not fall, but ascend. Heaven, gentlemen, is not shot through with orbiting machines. There is no happy hunting ground. You had it, once, but it's gone now, and that, Jack Tree, is what's written on your heart. The truth you have chosen to hide, even from yourself.

"The buffalo were doomed. You didn't need us. You didn't need us for war, or spite, or murder. Granted, we busted up your game something awful, but the four horses needed riders, and you rode them. I am here, and I see how the cold wind shakes each of you. The ghosts are dancing, my friends."

A cell buzzed at the stranger's hip. He snatched at it with a blue hand. William watched the blood pool in the man's torso, pulling away from the extremities. The man cupped a hand over the earpiece, listened, then nodded. He returned the phone to his belt.

"Fucking weather pattern sprung up out of nowhere. We've got a blow coming." He swung expressionless eyes on William. "A fucking bad one."

"They won't stay at home any longer," William said, smiling at Jack Tree. "They're coming with you. I'm sorry about that, but they refuse to be forgotten. Not now, not again."

"William," Daniel said earnestly, "you'd better come with us."

"We dug them up," William said, still watching Jack Tree. The hypothermia was far too rapid; it was a freezing of the soul. "Excavations. We found those forgotten stories. The mammoths, Dire Wolves, the short-tailed bears and smilodons, the bison antiquus. We found them all, rediscovered their lives and their deaths and it was all there in front of us. A story it wasn't politically expedient to read." William finally turned his attention to Daniel.

"This isn't a condemnation, Daniel. It's an embrace. Not so different after all. Human. Just human. A return to the old ways is a return to the wrong ways. I'm very sorry for that. It seemed so pristine. Paradise, but the nations had been birthed, the plains flooded with hunters on horseback, and the buffalo lost their final sanctuary—the deep plains. You already had your us and them. You were on your way, well on your way."

"Jesus," Daniel breathed, "It's freezing out here. This storm, Max, we talking snow?"

"Fucking ice age, Danny. This will slow us down, the last thing we need."

"No," William said, his tone bringing all three around. "The pillar must rise. Daniel, hear my words, now, before the feast. Your vision is true. I'll not hinder you. The storm is my legion, and I will lead it around you." William smiled suddenly and winked at Max. "The eye-spies still up there are old ones—they will be blind for days. Come now, come with all your technology, your workers, your supplies and set your genius to work."

William raised his arms, then turned to face the bitter wind. After a moment he began walking, along the ridge, eastward, away from the valley. He felt the three deathly cold men study his back, measuring his movements, wondering at the sudden falling off of the wind.

## NOAC NET:

"Behold, the hour cometh, yea, is now come, that ye shall be scattered, every man to his own," the Securicom official went on say. Recent reports that a third surveillance satellite has been sabotaged will not be confirmed by Securicom. The official described the present investigation as close to achieving the "cessation of terrorist activities", adding that the full measure of law enforcement will be vigorously expressed in the subduction of the terrorists...

...beneath the storm's cover. Unconfirmed reports indicate that construction at the new Ladon Site is now underway. A press release deemed "grossly incomplete" by NOAC and NUN representatives, issued yesterday by Ladon Inc. reveal that the project's chief engineer is Maxwell Ohman (a continuation of that posting from the Boxwell site), a man believed to be the Lady's lover...

...admitted that the trade sanctions against the Lakota Nation are "riddled with defiance on the part of free-standing corporations, unaligned nations, and Third World peripheral groups." The Minister went on to say that "health conditions in the closed nation are cause for gravest concern. On humanitarian reasons alone, NUN would be fully justified in direct military intervention."

NUN Security Council member Elias Ruby has denied the veracity of the Minister's claim, and repeated the Council's position on military intervention: "The EET (Extraordinary Economic Tribunal) has concluded that direct intervention between an unaligned nation and a corporation it has contracted with is permitted under very strict, clearly outlined circumstances. As of yet, neither Ladon nor Lakota Nation has breached any of these conditions."

At a second press conference the Minister refuted both the Security Council's and the EET's position. "I am very sorry, but if this project hasn't direct military application potential, I don't know what does. It seems clear that those very world organisations in place to protect us have been collectively cowed by the might of a single corporation and a single people. My God, what next?"

... One soweth, and another reapeth...

... lifted up the serpent in the wilderness as this Lady gazes upon the works of men, and sees before her the shape of a wheel that covers the valley, where within this circle are laid down spokes; this wheel that she sees sets now upon her lips the name giveth by the wise men who hunt no more: Medicine Wheel.

The axle will turn. It will pierce the heart of heaven.

... LADON: Greek, a mythological dragon that encircles the Tree of Life.

## NET HAPPYNEWS:

The formal entrance to the lifts leading down into the NUN Central Complex in Brussels was bioflicked yesterday at 5:10 PM local time. The dispersal agent is yet to be identified, but the toxic mix is confirmed as containing neurotoxins. Confirmed dead is at 175, including the suspect.

At the moment, investigators are unable to explain how the terrorist managed to elude in-place detection systems...

Communications worldwide have been disrupted by joystick terrorists working in concert on behalf of Ladon Inc. and the Lakota Nation. "The in-built firewall defences on comsats are notoriously outdated and ineffective," said a NOACom representative on condition of anonymity...

Seized tanker attempting to enter San Francisco Harbour contained 212 New Jihad terrorists and weapons including four SINJO-made tactical nukes. The New Jihad Organisation is a non-religious fanatic group (known colloquially as NERFS) with no known manifesto, although most members are recruited from refugee populations resettled from inundated Pacific islands...

## NET:

LUNKER:
This is getting out of hand, gentlemen.
VORPAL:
So there's blood on our hands. We have killed, I admit it, but it was in the service of a greater good.

LUNKER:
You seem so sure of yourselves, but dammit, this isn't the way it's supposed to be.
VORPAL:
You must be kidding, Lunker. There's some nasty trackers after us. We're just trying to stay alive.
LUNKER:
Look, stop using weather sats for your pinballing. They're big, and they come all the way down. If that's not bad enough, wait till some unmapped hurricane rolls across some unsuspecting atoll...
VORPAL:
Conventional options still exist. All right, I'll slow down some, get more selective.
LUNKER:
Thanks. Where's Blanc Knight?
VORPAL:
On the run. He started breaching Securicom Net Defenses, making haywire. He's busted down every secure system on the line. Man, you wouldn't believe the information spewing out.
LUNKER:
Bound For Ur reports NUN aircraft invading Lakota airspace, but being turned back by one helluva snow storm. The word goes on and says the project's ahead of schedule. Does that make any sense at all? Yeesh.
VORPAL:
Two unmanned spy-shuttles collided over Eastern Iowa. Crossed wires in the flight control data—don't fret, no ground injuries. That storm's circling the Hole right now, so I imagine NOAC will get the go-ahead for unilateral ground reccee from NUN. Wonder what they'll see?

## Entry: American N.W. 8 July A.C. 14

Sitting Bull crouched beside the hub of stones. The white sky made the prairie grass silver on the knoll, pewter in the valleys. The rifle sat on his lap, redhawk feathers hanging straight down and slowly spinning.

William walked up to the ancient ghost. "It was supposed to be a level playing field, Sitting Bull. Information was God, we rode the highway of His back. We rebelled against secrecy, but the revolution was illusory, wasn't it." He sat down beside the ghost. "All they did was change the meaning of words. Freedom meant forbidden. Access meant denial. Sitting Bull, I won't accept the lie. They called the dead a living memory, but it isn't. I've discovered that, now."

The Lakota chief squinted skyward. "I have never been a follower, William. All those ghosts in your wake, it's a path I can't take."

"I don't think God is inside liquid crystal," William said. "I don't think He superconducts, either. He doesn't ride fibre optics. I've begun to believe our faith is misplaced, Sitting Bull. We don't need more information. We need enlightenment."

Sitting Bull swung his empty gaze on William. "Species die, William. And yes, our hand has been in it, as far back as you could think to go."

William nodded. "To the days when we all lived in Africa, black-skinned under our wiry hair. The upright primate's God-given right. Maybe we came from Mars, fleeing the first world we fucked up. Maybe we didn't. It doesn't matter. What I want to know is: when did God finally recognise His own face in ours? Fifty million years ago? Five million years ago? A million? When did the light really dawn, Sitting Bull? Answer me that, please."

"Do you hold all life sacred, William?"

"Hell no," he answered. "HIV-37 sacred? The CFS nanoviral group? Pneumonic plague?" William studied the clouds overhead. "Life isn't sacred. If it is, we're all going to hell."

Sitting Bull smiled. "We already have, friend. Isn't that your message?"

"I have a message? Writing letters from the Hole doesn't stake any claim to prophecy."

"Ahh, I see," Sitting Bull was nodding. "You have doubts."

William pulled a crinkled layer of skin from his left hand and held it up to the sun's broken light. "I've realised something." He looked at the chief. "Culpability's not something you grow out of, is it?"

"Don't speak to me of regrets, son." Sitting Bull turned away, scanned the nearby ridge of hills. After a long moment he said, "Those thoughts can consume a soul, William. And in the end, what's the point? You hold the weasel in your hands until its twisting and squirming is known to you absolutely. The time comes to let it go."

"I'm tired," William said as he released the sheath of skin and watched it flutter away in the breeze. "Tired of seeking enlightenment. I no longer believe in that light turning on in your head. It's a myth. There's no discernible process, no sudden eureka. Such realisations are well after the fact, because when it happens, you're too busy to notice."

"Busy?"

William shrugged. "Preoccupied, then. Those brutal necessities of the flesh, the tortured schisms of the spirit. Busy. Busy screaming, busy bleeding, busy flailing at a host of memories and echoes and dead voices and faces that never were but come to you anyway and you can never, never peel them back."

Water dripped from Sitting Bull's hollow eyes. He ran his weathered, blunt-fingered hand along the barrel of his rifle. "Swift flight, the rifle ball flies unseen, yet strikes at the heart of things all the same. I heard your words to Jack Tree. They broke him."

"I know."

"We would have slain all the bison. Pte Oyate, Buffalo Nation. In the manner that our ancestors slew all the bison antiquus, the very first Tatanka. We would have continued to war on our neighbours, and those wars would have grown, and the blood of feuds would run like the river. We would have gutted the horse of our brother, rather than see it run beyond our grasp. But, William, that history would have been ours, and ours alone. You broke us too soon, left us unmindful of the consequences of our own actions, you left us believing the buffalo would once again cover the plains, and you left us with a belief in our hearts that our hands were clean. For this, William, I can never forgive you."

"So is Jenine MacAlister right, then? You're all still children, after all, still unblooded in the ways of inevitability, tottering on the edge of extinction simply because you refuse to adapt, or you're not able to adapt, because you need guidance in growing up. Am I supposed to believe all that bullshit?"

Sitting Bull smiled. "Our ways are different, William. They are children, yes, but they are my children. Do you think my eternal guidance insufficient? Think on this, son: we spirits whisper lessons to our children; from all that we have seen and all that we were, we tell our children this one thing: there is no such thing as inevitability."

"What makes you so sure?"

"In the way Mother adapts, in the way she refuses to surrender." Sitting Bull raised his rifle and sighted down its length. "In my days, the white men and Indian alike gathered the buffalo skulls beside the tracks of the iron horse. We piled them into mountains. They were taken away, and ground up into fertiliser. The fertiliser was used in the breaking of the prairie soil so that crops could be planted, and so the buffalo returned to the earth, and gave forth life."

"Your irony's a little too bitter for me, friend."

"In your words, then, William. Nature revises. She is each life and she is all life, and so she will outlive us all."

"There's secret reports," William said. "Data compiled on the Inside populations—inside the rad shields, inside the cities and complexes. The trends are alarming. Increased toxemia across the board, dropping fertility—inactive, sluggish sperm in low numbers, impermeable ova, toxic lactation syndrome, chronic respiratory diseases, a whole host of immuno-deficiency disorders. Projections bring to mind the fate of the Neanderthal in Europe when faced with what could've been as little as a 0.5% differential in infant mor-tality rates, when compared with the emerging true humans. Ten thousand years and complete displacement, absolute extinction."

"Who waits in the wings this time?" Sitting Bull asked.

William smiled at the Lakota chief. "You already know. Peripheral populations. Pressured populations. Are you ready for that, Sitting Bull? To look upon your children and see that their faces are no longer a match to yours?"

The old man thumbed back the flintlock and squinted as he aimed. "Where I am, these ghost buffalo seem real. I still take pleasure in hunting them."

"Meaning?"

"Meaning, William, that my face isn't the face of God." He squeezed the trigger.

The loud report echoed dully across the valley.

―᠊ᨆ᠊―

NOACom:
    FREEDOM FILES REQUIRE CLEARANCE. WHO IS THIS, PLEASE?
JOHN JOHN:
    ********
NOACom:
    Welcome to Freedom Files. This information block complies with all New United Nations charters and conventions. Proceed with Query.
JOHN JOHN:
    University of Saskatchewan, Applied Sciences Ministry, Department of Anthropology\student field projects\summer A.C. 14.

NOACom:
> Seven graduate field projects are listed. Six are sponsored by USask Board of Funding. One is through private funding. List?

JOHN JOHN:
> Private funding only.

NOACom:
> Potts, William. Project Description unavailable.

JOHN JOHN:
> Student File, Potts, William.

NOACom:
> Please note: Student File, Potts, William, is docked with Securicom. Proceed?

JOHN JOHN:
> Yes.

NOACom:
> Password?

JOHN JOHN:
> ...

NOACom:
> Password?

JOHN JOHN:
> *M*A*L*A*C*H*A*I

NOACom:
> Good evening, Dean Roberts.

JOHN JOHN:
> Open file, please.

NOACom:
> Potts, William, student number 5257525
> Department of Anthropology, Graduate Studies.
> Family status (last updated A.C.12):
> > Deceased parent:
> > > Berman Potts, PhD,
> > > Mathematics
> > Deceased parent:

    Lucinda nee Bolen, PhD,
    Biology
  Deceased sibling:
    John (elder)
    (leukaemia, 2011)
  Deceased sibling:
    Arthur (twin, SIDS, 1987)
Course History:
  Pertinent to field of study:
    Intro. Applied Anthro 0:01
    Applied Anthro 0:02
    Culture Dynamics 0:02
    Social Evolution 0:02
    Extinction Dynamics 0:02
    Systems Theory in Anthro 0:03
    Processual Anthro 0:03
    Revised History of Anthro 0:04
  Additional studies:
    Biological Ethics 0:01
    Systems Theory in Gov't (required)
    Communications (required)
    History of the Oral Tradition
    Semantics (required)*
    Genetics and the Mind
    Advanced Systems Theory (required)*
    Advanced Communications (required)
    Models of Multiculturalism*
     * denotes incomplete

| Major Papers: | Grade: |
|---|---|
| Ethics in Systems Theory | (sat) |
| Communicating Knowledge | (sat) |
| Rewiring the Mind (brain function and instinct) | (sat) |
| The Evolution of Fieldwork | (fail) |

  Unpredictability in Systems Theory  (fail)
Failures:
 revision required, status pending
Grant Applications:
 Category:
 Fieldwork
 Project:
  Rural Waysides: Subjects who are Non-Participants in Social Programming: Case Studies
 Accepted:
  affirmative
 Project:
  Hole Peripheral Occupation:
  Case Studies of Occupants Living on the Periphery of the Midwest Hole.
 Accepted:
  conditional
 Project:
  Lakota Adaptations to the Midwest Hole
 Accepted:
  negative*
   * Applicant succeeded in acquiring permission from the Lakota Nation with signatory: Horn, D., Exec Band Council.

 Project:
  Unknown (private grant)*
  * Wheel Foundation

Potts, William is listed as a Subversive Class 01 (potential). The following observation reports are compiled from academic observation reports (aor), field operatives, E-surveillance.

AOR (course instructors & required Report Review Committee):
a) Subject displays an exceptional level of inquisitiveness.
b) Subject takes perverse pleasure in challenging accepted applications of social theory.
c) Subject is advanced in communications theory applications.
d) Subject's father is a known dissident for which Subject displays incorrect pride.
e) Subject displays advanced (unapproved) knowledge of Numbers Theory and Chaos Theory (Chaos Theory is Suppressed Information, See Freedom File 210X210). Assume Parental Education, contravening NOAC Parenting Parameters, Criminal Code 16-21IIa)-f).
f) Subject employed No-Trace variants on Net, using a Remote Fieldbook.
g) Subject continually disrupted classes with adversarial interrogatives.
h) Subject identified two assigned field operatives via Valentine Cards with boxed chocolates (chocolates analysed and cleared)
i) Subject displayed advanced knowledge of technological engineering Systems Theory & application.
j) Subject revealed knowledge of pre-revised archaeology and anthropological dynamics.
k) Subject revealed knowledge of Indigenous Peoples' History, Mythology & Belief Systems prior to Applied Anthropological Restructuring of Said Peoples.
l) Subject successfully breached this file with insufficient trail to advance criminal proceedings.
Present Net Entries: Unavailable.

JOHN JOHN:
Delete File, Potts, William.
NOACom:
This file is docked at Securicom. There are no other copies of this file, as per Securicom Subversive Investigations Parameters. Do you still wish to Delete?
JOHN JOHN:
Yes.
NOACom:
File Deleted.
JOHN JOHN:
Delete File, Potts, Berman. Potts, Lucinda n. Bolen
NOACom:
No such file exists.
JOHN JOHN:
Sniff back.
NOACom:
File, Potts, Berman, File, Potts, Lucinda nee Bolen were accidentally destroyed in Data Transfer, A.C. 13. Investigation ongoing: sabotage suspected.
JOHN JOHN:
Delete Ongoing Investigation Data File, Data Transfer A.C. 13, Potts, Berman & Lucinda.
NOACom:
File Deleted.
JOHN JOHN:
Delete all Subversive all Classes Files.
NOACom:
Working. All files deleted, Subversive all Classes Files. 16174.96 QTB now available in Securicom System.
JOHN JOHN:
Delete all E-surveillance Files.
NOACom:
Working...

# NET:

**STONECASTER:**

A modest query, then. How is it that he's getting clearer? Hours tick into days out under that deadly sun. The boy's cooked, his skin peeling, half-blind.

**CORBIE TWA:**

Into and out of, Stony. Clarity's the word all right. Crystal clear. He's pushed through. He's been cleansed, hell, reborn to the hour.

**STONECASTER:**

Still kind of suspicious to my thinking.

**BOGQUEEN:**

Your thinking's still too linear, Stonecaster. He's on a seasonal round, moving a cyclical route. When I read him, I feel him orbiting out there, coming round and round, coming closer with each pass of the great wheel. The closer he gets to what he's been circling, the clearer things become. For him, for us.

**PACEMAKER:**

This last hint of NOAC data on population projections and biological dynamics has me curious, to say the least. I wonder if such data exist, and if the trend projections lead to certain inevitable conclusions.

**CORBIE TWA:**

Carefully crafted belief systems acquire a power of their own. Methinks the powers that be are bucklin under an imperative of their own makin. Inertia's set in, and now that new information's comin down the line and mussin up their coiffs, they can't do nothin but lean into the wind.

**BOGQUEEN:**

Political structures don't adapt, they react. None of this should surprise you.

PACEMAKER:
There are others out there, like us, who have declared war. It's a war of information, the staccato of data on all sides. And some have taken a step further down the combative line.
CORBIE TWA:
Ah, you must mean the terrorists.
PACEMAKER:
Strictly speaking, that's exactly what they are. Not that I'm complaining. The walls of silence have been breached, and data spills like blood into our hands.
CORBIE TWA:
How poetic. But I think the reality's a tad messier than that, Pacemaker. These guys are pulling down satellites.
LUNKER:
That has, I believe, tailed off lately. For the simple reason that NOAC and the rest have laid off harassing Ladon Inc. and the Lakota.
PACEMAKER:
Given that cyclical stormfront over the Central Plains, they haven't much choice. Now that their hi-tech see-all microsats are all gone...
BOGQUEEN:
Around and around he circles...
STONECASTER:
You can't be serious, Bogqueen. Leave me out if you're going mystical on us. The boy's an opportunist.
FREE WHIZZY:
All very interesting, ladies and gents, but I can't help feeling these aimless musings are essentially pointless. We need to get organised. We need a list of things to do, things that arise from a set of goals. There's an ocean of previously restricted information out there. The boy's dropping enough crumbs. Time for us to start sniffing the trails.
CORBIE TWA:
You seriously think William knows what he's doing? That

he's callin for our help? That he has some kind of grand scheme to bring the world to its knees?

FREE WHIZZY:

He may not be consciously aware of such motives, Corbie Twa. Nevertheless, they are clearly operant, no matter who, or what the source.

CORBIE TWA:

Divine guidance?

BOGQUEEN:

You said it, not us.

STONECASTER:

The boy's dragged you all with him, hasn't he? Right into the quagmire of madness. Raving loons in the Swamp.

FREE WHIZZY:

You're free to surface at will, Stonecaster. No one's insisting you remain.

CORBIE TWA:

Calm down, everyone. Look, somethin's drawn us to William's net entries. All of us, Stonecaster included. We don't know nothin at all about William, when it comes right down to it. An untreated psychotic? Megalomaniac? Or just someone who knows too much—

BOGQUEEN:

We're not completely ignorant, Corbie. William dances this Swamp like a whirling dervish. He evades every tracking effort, slips through every drift-net NOAC's dragging across the waves. He's accessed restricted information and tosses us conceptual time-bombs. Is he sitting back right now and laughing while we desperately juggle?

CORBIE TWA:

You forget one thing, lass. He's dyin of rad poisonin and toxemia. And he walked into that of his own free will. That, to my mind, seriously undermines his authority as a revolutionary thinker.

STONECASTER:
> Unless it's all a scam. What if he's driving around out there in some NOAC-issue rad buggy. Throwing us timebombs all right, then laughing when they explode in our faces.

PACEMAKER:
> This speculation serves nothing. I believe Free Whizzy's desire to organise is worthwhile. For one, I am interested in pursuing these population projection data. Much might be unveiled there, about both William and the Official Domain.

LUNKER:
> Some of my associates are already working certain related areas. They are actively widening the cracks in the official wall. I'll lay out a thread down to this place, and pertinent information shall surely find you.

PACEMAKER:
> Thank you.

JOHN JOHN:
> Hello one and all. Open a cubby, ladies and gentlemen, while I toss you all some background data on one Potts, William. I'm afraid I can't stick around and chat. There's a few more things that I need to do. Stay together, keep talking—you may not know it, but your silent audience is vast, and the threads... they fall toward you like rain...

# Five

American N.W. Terminal Zone, 11 July, A.C. 14

They gathered beneath a tarp that flapped drum-like in the wind. Seated on folding chairs around a three-legged metal table covered in fine lace. High-electrolyte drinks served from a refractive decanter. Beneath their feet a thick, broad rug.

On all sides on the hilltop the big and little bluestems fluttered their flowers like butterflies pinned to a board. Western wheatgrass and green needle shivered their feathery stalks. Blades and stems all sharp-edged now, reflective juices glittering and defying absorption, shunting deadly rad into the buffered earth. Impervious flowers that opened like throats at dusk and gusted out clouds of pollen that drifted in air swarming with flitting insects.

Bundles of sage smouldered around the periphery of the tarp's shadow, streams of smoke spiralling and spinning away on the wind. The sage leaves, thicker than leather, burned with an inner fuel, an expulsion of energy as slow and steady as its previous absorption. A balance mocking the chemical descent into ashes.

William squatted just beyond the shadow, at the crest of the western slope where the cacti spread out and down the sun-drenched hillside in mauve and dusty green. Needles angled in antithesis to ancient sunflowers, away from the sun's light. The symbiotic spiders had spun a mane of angel hair down the entire slope, glistening false dew like a dense scatter of diamonds. The spiders fed on cactus mites through the night, their webs full of cactus spores and tugged away by the scuttling passage of mice and needle-beaked birds that still hopped from pod to pod, plucking flower buds and drinking succulent juices. A microcosm of dependency, newly achieved—to William, a miracle, a creation so precise, so wonderful, that he felt it light his being.

Daniel Horn watched Jack Tree light the pipe. The young man's face hinted at irony, a delicious taste at the back of his thoughts.

Max Ohman, the Lady's representative, leaned back in his chair, both hands holding the glass of lime-coloured liquid on his lap. Where his eyes held, behind the sunglasses, William couldn't guess. They may well have been closed, for all the rest of his face betrayed.

Doctor Jenine MacAlister sat opposite the three men, studying a hand-held notebook with the view-screen draped in the shadow of her right hand. She had been reading the stress data for some time now. Finally she glanced up at Max Ohman. "The tensile properties are clearly best-case scenario, Max. What kind of in-field tests have you conducted?"

Max cleared his throat. "Eleven years, Doctor. We in-field tested in Saudi Arabia, at Boxwell Plateau, and of course at the source-point orbiting station. As of this morning, we have extended the tether-lines thirty-six kilometers from the station, well into the ionosphere. A free-flying test-run. The stress factors are more than satisfactory. The tensile properties are not best-case, they're actual. When I say this poly-ore matrix bends, I mean exactly that, Doctor. It bends."

Jenine closed the notebook's screen lid and reached for her glass. "Of course I'll need to send the structural details to our NOAC specialists."

Max Ohman's grin was coldly feral. "Like hell you will, Doctor. Unless you've got an optic implant or eidetic memory, that data remains the property of Ladon Corporation. And," he continued in a droll tone, "our file on you indicates neither implants nor eidetic memory."

Jenine let it drop. Just another smokescreen. William watched her, saw her mind work, and knew her soul. All so clear, now.

"What remains unspoken," Jack Tree said, repacking the pipe he'd yet to pass to anyone, "is what has brought us here. I think the time for true words has begun."

Jenine leaned back and steepled her fingers, elbows perched on the arms of the chair. A gesture William had seen a thousand times. A gesture of lies and secret contempt. "Very well. First of all, to whom do I speak? You, Jack, or Daniel Horn?"

Jack Tree looked away, his eyes squinting as he gazed out across the valley.

"Begin any time," Daniel Horn said. He wouldn't let her narrow her targeting. If she had hidden knives of a personal sort, the kind of information NOAC operatives loved to collect, she'd have to throw them at all three men. Made wounding random, and of uncertain efficacy. No leverage here, Jenine.

"NOAC has NUN approval for the following pre-emptive actions, gentlemen. I make that clear now, should you believe—erroneously—that your foes are not united on this matter. We are absolutely united." She paused, tracking her severe expression across all three faces opposite her. A conscious gesture, almost mechanical. She'd practised, but not enough, not nearly enough.

"We're not illiterate, Doctor," Daniel said. "You're united on nothing. Major crises in Southeast Asia, the Indian subcontinent, the Middle East, Ukraine, South Africa—the whole damn game's blowing up in your faces, and that's not even mentioning the economic mess. Now, do go on, Doctor."

"Stealth strikes," Jenine snapped. "Full ground incursion with punitive objectives. Oil fields reclaimed, mineral rights on all lands acquired by your peoples retracted once the areas are secured." She scanned the faces again, this time more successfully. "Any attempt to resist these missions will be met with the full retaliatory might of NOAC military force. Your people will die, gentlemen."

Max Ohman barked, "Justification?"

Jenine smiled. "Our major concern is for the safety of all indigenous peoples in the Midwest, and all citizen populations of the North American Confederacy who have been assessed as at risk from the Medicine Wheel Project. Your stress data is in my opinion flawed—"

"Since when did you become an engineer?" Max asked, his teeth still bared.

"My opinion has been granted authority, Mr. Ohman."

"By whom?"

"NOAC and NUN have placed me in the primary position as negotiator in these proceedings."

"Big effing deal," Max said. "You may have authority in some kind of illusory political sense, but I was challenging your opinion. Crunch some numbers for me, Doctor. Show me the flaws in the equations. Would you like pad and paper? Us engineers still use those, you know."

"You, Mr. Ohman," Jenine said coolly, "have been granted the privilege of attending this meeting as an observer. That is a privilege I am empowered to retract at any time."

Max snorted and looked away.

"Now," Jenine resumed, "where was I?"

"Killing my people in order to save them," Daniel Horn said.

"More than just your people are in danger," Jenine said. "NOAC is responsible to its citizens—"

"Since when?" Max asked.

She ignored him, and continued. "We are obliged to protect them from unwarranted risks, arising from either corporate activities, or external political instability."

Daniel asked softly, "Are you suggesting that my position as head of the Lakota Nation is inherently unstable?"

"Your recent actions in concert with Ladon Corporation have suggested this, Mr. Horn."

"Your ultimatum?" Daniel asked.

"Close down the project immediately. The sanctions will be lifted, and normal relations can resume."

"Doctor MacAlister," Daniel began, leaning forward, "you more than anyone must know that my people and your people have never had normal relations. As for sanctions, you have maintained the imposition of the most insidious kinds of sanctions for five hundred years and counting. Do you actually imagine that you can still hurt us?"

Jack Tree spoke, "Kill us, yes, by all means. What is a few more scars on your conscience?"

"She can't," Max said. "Her threats are sheer bluff. Every peripheral nation in the world is watching this play out. Secondary and primary nations are grid-locked on this, politically and philosophically. Protests and riots are erupting in one major city after another. It's all falling apart, all because one lone independent nation said 'yes' to the dream."

Jack Tree said, "You were so certain, Doctor, weren't you? Convinced by all your covert anthropological data. You thought the dream-times were dead. You've plied us with schemes designed to make us invisible, even to ourselves. You called it the application of successful adaptive cultural adjustment. For all your efforts to save us by destroying us, we have still defied you. We have met our dream." He paused and studied the steatite pipe in his hands. "Not, I'll grant you, in the way I would have imagined it. The pattern in the skies is new to me, so new that it sometimes frightens me. But I am old, my days are almost done. What I pass on to my children is and always will be the one thing you cannot control, cannot shape to suit your ends. My gift is the history of the damned, and my poison is truth. You see, Doctor, I remember."

Jenine said, "You're all making a terrible mistake."

"If we are," Daniel said, "it will be ours, not yours. Possessing something—even freedom—is two-edged. Our days of sucking at your collective tit are over. The time's come for you to let go." He smiled, and it was a smile of sad wisdom. "I had hoped for your blessing, for the cleansing of your hands. But no, you still try to possess us. If it comforts you to call that possession something else, like protection, compassion, or a justifiable maternal instinct, then so be it. Whatever word you choose, it still means chains to us."

Entry: American N.W. 11 July, 2014

"Enough of the preliminaries," Jenine said, "let's get to negotiating this treaty."

Jack Tree repacked his pipe and set a burning ember to the steatite bowl. "We have come to listen, Doctor MacAlister."

"As representative of the North American Confederacy and spokesperson for the divine will of the Triumvirate of A.C. 14, I am authorised to negotiate the honourable purchase of the following items from those gathered here as representatives of the Lakota Nation and related sovereign peoples of the Midwest Hole; said representatives being thusly identified and duly recorded: John 'Jack' Tree Whose Roots are Deep, and Daniel Horn, of the Lakota Nation. Do you acknowledge your presence here at this gathering?"

"We do."

"Excellent, we're off to a fine start that will benefit us all. We are, as you know, newcomers to your lands, granted by right of God and King, and by right of Manifest Destiny to rule over and subjugate all peoples we encounter should they prove incapable of opposing us. Regardless of our motive, our methods remain singular in their objective: to wit, either by direct violent action upon the persons of said indigenes, or by systematic destruction of their habitat and subsistence patterns, or by insipid destruction of their social fabric and way of life as categorised by cultural affiliation, through such deus ex machina vectors as disease, alcohol, enforced indoctrination of our religious beliefs, legal removal of children for purposes of education and assimilation, restriction to peripheral lands unsuitable to sustaining traditional lifestyles and conducive to general cultural deterioration through long-term programs to ensure dependency, loss of dignity, removal of personal responsibility in matters of familial care, education, sustenance procurement, shelter maintenance, and so on.

"Toward the satisfactory completion of our singular goal, we are herewith purchasing from those in attendance and those peoples they represent, the following: your land, your life.

"In return, and as payment for the above, we offer you one hundred million buffalo skulls, the rusted hulks of five hundred thousand combines, desiccated farms, diseases, substance abuse, dependency, structured lives, hand-outs, starvation, hatred, loss of intellectual and spiritual property, identity, will, dignity, and pride. Sign here, please."

"No."

"I am empowered to offer the following as further incentive. Complete biological data on peripheral population and projections leading to the inevitable conclusion: to wit, within six generations those populations centred in the secondary and primary civilisations, characterised by protective measures of extreme technological life-sustaining intervention, will become extinct as a species, due primarily to pressure and displacement by a new speciation of the homo sapien hominid lineage, which will arise in pressured environments commonly found among peripheral populations, such as yours.

"In exchange for this data, we request intensive biological analysis of your peoples over the next century, including the right to blood and protective properties thereof, including rad resistant properties, vaccine and serum potential, immunodefence systems against toxemia and related syndromes, new organs and new properties of organs, neurological developments and all genetic traits determined to be conducive to species survival. In short, we ask for your life. We'll worry about the land later."

"It seems," Daniel Horn said, "that your Manifest Destiny possesses a heretofore unknown appendix, wherein lies the inevitable conclusion, a conclusion you have espoused as wholly natural: species extinction. Unfortunately, the species about to become extinct is your own."

"You do not understand our desperation."

"I do now, Doctor MacAlister."

"Will you help us? Will you save us?"

"In the manner you have just described, no, we won't help you."

"But don't you see? We have bled for you. For five hundred years we have bled for you, for what we did to you."

"That blood is unhealthy, Doctor. Do you grasp my meaning?"

"Whatever happened to reciprocity?"

"It lives on, but it was never what you believed it to be. You saw it with a scientist's eyes, Doctor, so you saw wrong. I'm not really interested in explaining it to you, Doctor. William has come to understand, finally. You might want to ask him."

"He tells me nothing."

"Nothing you want to hear."

"Will you help us, Daniel? A few drops of blood? The conveyance of your dead?"

"We'll think about it, Doctor."

---

American N.W. Midwest Hole, 14 July, A.C. 14

The coyotes streamed down the hillside, driven from their invisible places and becoming four distinct mercurial shapes parting the high magenta grasses. They reached the dry riverbed then scattered. William blinked, and they were gone.

Somewhere behind him rose a ragged slope, lifting the earth into an undercut cresting wave that hung frozen over the flat sweeps of sand and silt. Its shadow slowly crawled across him. He remembered standing on the ridge, the earth giving under him, a heavy, bruising fall.

His backpack lay a dozen meters away, resting against a tuft of grass. The flap had torn, and he saw a liquid glint of metal in the darkness within.

It felt over. The journey cut short, incomplete. He didn't have the strength to get up.

He'd seen into the coyotes, read their new imperatives like blushes of red behind their eyes. Opportunists, newly aggressive and far too clever for comfort. When night came, they too would come.

Life's cycles are flavoured with irony. They've been following me, following the scent of blood, and in an hour they'll come to close the book. Patient bastards. What's ten thousand years, after all?

He stared at the object inside his backpack, the clarity of his thinking almost too bitter to bear.

Someone had challenged planetary laws. Semipermeable, pliable polysteel that shunted friction like water off a seal's back, turned heat into static—a hundred trillion threads a single molecule thick, each kilometres long, accommodating stress factors in the nano-bloodstream of carbon corpuscles. When I say it bends, I mean it bends, Doctor.

The laws dictated equatorial placement: rotational imperatives. Ladon tried acquiring it. Rivals and nations caught wind and went to the New United Nations. Before long, they'd hammered so many legal spikes into the equation Ladon couldn't buy a bucket of dirt if it came from the equator. They had no choice but to look elsewhere, and to challenge toe to toe the exigencies of rotational dynamics.

It took eleven years before the Lady and Max Ohman stood atop the mountain, raised high the stone tablet, then swung it shattering down. Not an elevator as much as a slide, the tail of a spermatozoa, slanting skyward. Another miracle of engineering tethering it in place.

Nobody should reach that high. Frail humans should never strive for godhood. The wax melts, justice is meted out. Exaltation is suspect. Anybody with balls like that deserves to get them chopped off. They stand so tall their shadows cover the world, and us frail humans begrudge the loss of light upon our upturned faces.

Not that we ever paid any attention to it when it showered down its brilliant promise.

But never mind that.

Nobody should reach that high. No matter the quagmire of emotions drowning in insipid fears and flaws, no matter the primal pit of terror bubbling uneasy beneath those words. It was a statement voiced the world over, there in those shadows cast down by achievement. Sometimes a whine, mostly vicious with blind, unreasoning hatred. The unspoken secret remained: what the shadows hid was darkness in the soul, and its voice was spite, and it said: Nobody should reach that high.

Well, Ladon reached, was reaching even now. It seemed the world was having trouble living with that fact.

An hour before dusk. Maybe less. William continued staring at the object in the backpack. He felt sickness in his flesh, something like a fever, but somehow sour as well. A taste of corruption.

The ghosts were gone. He'd sent them off, riding the storm as it tracked the blistered lands of the Hole. He hoped one would come back in time, one in particular. He'd not seen that one yet, but he was sure it was there, somewhere in the army of dead that had dogged his tracks.

A sound off to his right, footsteps crunching through the crust of calcined sand. And beyond that—William now heard—the hum of a rover's engine.

"Oh hell," William mumbled through broken lips. "I thought it was over."

"The Lord have mercy," Old Jim breathed softly as he crouched down beside William Potts. "Unpack the kit, Stel, I figure he's taken more than seventy MRs for every day he's been out here, never mind the dehydration, sun and wind burns and, hell, starvation."

Stel handed Old Jim the medikit. Her gaze remained on William as she tried remembering what he'd looked like, that night in his room. Gaunt even then, but this. She barely recognised him.

"He'll need plasma," Old Jim said as he prepared a syringe. "Fluids."

"He needs clean marrow," Stel said.

"Better call the university. Tell 'em we're taking him back to Val Marie, and they'd better get someone over, fast."

Old Jim's weathered hands worked over William, stripping back the ragged bootsuit. He knew there were questions that Stel wanted answered. Questions about how he'd driven all over the damn place, about how he'd found the boy. The Hole was a big place, after all. The chances of finding him were damn near hopeless.

He injected William with E-67 flushant, the latest available in rad treatment.

*How the hell can I tell her I had help? How can I tell her that I followed an old Indian ghost?*

"Let's get him in the buggy."

*Some goddamned ghost leading me across the prairie, an Indian ghost carrying a goddamn rifle slung with redhawk feathers.*

"Jim," Stel said.

He looked up and cursed the shadows that hid her face.

"Jim," Stel said again.

"What?"

She continued staring down on him a moment longer. Then she turned away. "I need a cigarette."

Jim drove steadily, his antiquated patrol buggy bouncing and jolting on its stiff shocks. It'd been years since the Palliser Triangle Survey, when he'd played chauffeur to a bunch of scientists. He remembered all the weather readings they took, and the soil and plant samples. Insect nets strung out between the tents at night; animal traps, bird snares, bat nets that looked like giant lobster traps. When it was all over, they rushed off to the university with all their goodies. Old Jim had gotten a six month bonus to his credit line, arthritis in his misaligned hip, and the solar-powered patrol buggy. Even with the crotchety hip, Jim figured he came out ahead in the deal.

Stel smoked in the seat beside him. William lay unconscious along the length of the back bench. The silence was as thick as the smoke.

Dusk had arrived, the sun spreading out on the west horizon like a copper lake. Helishuttles had been coming and going through the Hole for a week now. Jack Tree and his cronies were cooking something big along with that corporation. Somewhere out there on the dead lands. Old Jim's expression soured as he thought of Jack Tree. Too damn clever by far. One day he'll hear about my artifact collection, and come calling. He'll take it all. The law backs him. He'll take it all from me. All eight generations, swept away. Too goddamn clever by far.

"What're his chances?" Stel asked suddenly.

Jim shrugged. "Short term, he'll make it fine. Long term..." Jim shrugged again. He licked his lips, kept his eyes on the rolling plain in front of them. "Figure he's burned blind, though."

"Blind," Stel said. "Well, hell, what's to see these days anyway? Damned TV stations all losing it every ten bloody minutes, for Christ's sake. Al says it's those helishuttles. Remote-guided, he says, with a flight-path right over town screwing up transmissions or something."

"Oh yeah," Jim said, not really listening. Goddamned TVs who buys the shit they're saying anyway. World's gone to hell, ain't it just. He'd seen the latest shots of Iraq in the National Geographic.

Robot camera teams rolling through ancient ruins. Caption talked about it being the first city ever built. Talked about some King named Gilgamesh. The shots were eerie as hell. Red sky, all those cobbled roads and things exposed by the blown sands. And here and there the rusting hulks of tanks and trucks. Eerie because it all looked so normal, like the pictures were just waiting for someone to walk through, some kid herding goats or something. But nothing. Nuclear fallout still at lethal levels.

The first city was dead, would always be dead.

More shots, modern echoes in Iran. Black, burned-up bodies covering the streets, the squares, covering the steps leading up to slagged mosques. Not a bird, probably not even a bug. Even the Indian Ocean was half-dead, all the surface plankton incinerated in the multiple blasts, a yard of water stripped off the whole damn ocean.

Maybe the boy's onto something, after all. He's wearing the scars we keep running from. He knows we're running out of room. He knows we fucked it up, we're fucking it all up even now. Bloody wars, ninety million dead of starvation in Africa, Armageddon in Jerusalem, plague in China, Bombay carpet-bombed. Here I am trying to save a boy from rad poisoning. What the hell for?

"Heard the weather's coming back," Stel said, lighting a last cigarette as the old motel on the edge of town came into view.

"We're in a loop," Jim said. "Goes round and round."

Stel took a deep drag, released the smoke in an even stream. "Must be sun-spots or something."

Old Jim swung the buggy up onto the motel's cracked parking lot pavement. "Must be," he said.

---

They took William to his old room in the hotel. Stel washed him down, so gently it stung Jim's eyes to watch. When they had the boy laid out on the bed, Jim set up the plasma kit. Saline, electrolytes, anti-leukaemic compounds, lithium and more E-67. The standard rad treatment set-up, available in every peripheral town. With some old fart like me trained like a monkey. Mix this, drip that. Tap the vein, insert with a steady probing motion—you'll feel the venal wall when you puncture it. Bathe all solar burns in weak saline and E-67. Run the flush as soon as possible, and that means the catheter. If the victim's male...

Stel watched him for a few minutes, then headed to the door. "I'll buzz that woman who keeps calling for him. Guess she'll come and pick him up."

Jim nodded. After a moment he heard Stel leave.

"Oh, son," Jim said softly, sponging solution into William's swollen eyes. "Just like a sun dance, huh? Push past the pain, find that cool, peaceful place. Too bad you couldn't take your body with you."

---

He'd first shown up three years ago. Even then, as he started knocking on doors, slicking the locals at the pool table, and just being damn good at listening, Old Jim knew the boy had arrived with wide open eyes.

He'd cared about their lives. At first, it was some kind of philosophical caring. William bled for the idea of them. He came as a chronicler, but that first season changed him. The idea found faces, a score of faces. The caring changed, and when he looked in your eyes the glaze was gone. You could see him in his eyes, and he saw you, and it was a clear thing both ways.

One night, late at the hotel bar, William sat with a half dozen locals for hours on end. Old Jim had watched the layers crumble in the boy, watched as William was pushed deep into himself by the stories the old-timers threw around. They'd been talking about the changes.

"North of here," Aimes was saying, "where they grew canola and didn't do much ranching, well, I remember the fields just falling dead, toppling in waves. Next thing you know the sky's grey with locusts, come to eat the poisoned canola, right down to the ground." Aimes squinted down at the glass of beer in his rope-veined hands. "A hundred million, they said. A hundred million rotting locusts, the sky empty as the dawn of time..."

"We'd get the traffic coming down from Swift Current," Browning said. "On their way to those ski resorts in Montana. I saw one accident, shit—"

William cut in, his voice dull, "I know what's missing." He looked up, scanned the faces around him. Old Jim remembered the loss in the boy's eyes, remembered the way that look made his chest tighten. "I know what's missing here. There's no dogs."

"They died fast," Aimes said, nodding. "Cats just hid during the day, did the usual at night. But the dogs died for a long while there."

"I saw some litters make you upchuck your granma's meat-loaf," Browning said.

"I hear they're doing fine in the shielded cities," Old Jim said, trying to ease the anguish in William's face. Hell, he remembered thinking, they're just damn dogs. Don't compare to the skin cancers, the babies poisoned by breast milk and living the rest of their days inside plastic-bag rooms. Don't compare at all, dammit. Just dogs.

"There should be dogs," William said. "Barking like hell every time I walk into the yard. Challenging the stranger, doing their job for you people. Nobody's taken their place. You don't challenge anymore. You don't raise shit just to see what the stranger's made of. No stranger ever fooled a dog. Ever."

"That's a damn fact, that is," Browning said, nodding.

Old Jim stared at the boy. What you spill up tells a lot, but reaching the place where you'll do it in the company of old men, that tells a whole lot more.

William's outburst slipped away, into that timeless stream of gripes and bitches that filled the hours before dawn. He'd joined the town, that night. He'd shifted the place he looked at things from. He'd lined up with the peripherals, the subjects of his study, and saw the world in a new way that was in truth an old way. Maybe the oldest way of all.

A hell of a way to step out of being young. Probably the night that Stel decided she'd get him in her bed sooner or later. She wouldn't do that for a stranger. But she'd help a local boy get a bit older.

Help was something he drew to him. Halo'd Mary and an old Indian ghost.

NET:

FREE WHIZZY:
So NOAC's on its own. What do you make of the threats to invade? Anyone?
PACEMAKER:
Highly unlikely. They really banked on NUN approval, and it looked for a time there like they had it, but now it's all fallen apart.
LUNKER:
All the rats have scurried to the stern, eyes tilting up, way up. Salvation beckons.
CORBIE TWA:
Ladon's not selling. The Lakota are staying belligerent. Assembly is on schedule, the orbiting chute is in position, geosynchronous perfection. Fifth Floor, men's underwear...
LUNKER:
Can't get off what you can't get onto first, so the rats won't get a ride, no matter how much they squeal. It's kind of sweet, in a pathetic, pan-suicidal way.
PACEMAKER:
I've reviewed the population projection data and it seems William Potts is playing Pandora. This is highly alarming information.

BOGQUEEN:
Details, please.
PACEMAKER:
Very well, and bear in mind the data is no longer secured, it's riding a very accessible crest. I won't bore you with technical details, but the conclusions the top-dog geneticists have reached can be stated as follows.
One:
Pressured populations possess a greater likelihood of mutation that selects for successful adaptation to changing environments. Dynamics remain typically tautological, but the result is speciation—the emergence of a new species of hominid. Homo sapiens neosapien, whatever you want to call it. This speciation is rapid-fire, the so-called punctuated equilibrium hypothesis. Very fast in its definition process. It's happening now among certain peripheral populations—those groups who for whatever reason are outside civilised intervention in environmental management. The traits are highly variable among these groups, but they meet the definitive requirements: increased phenotype viability.
Two:
Central populations, defined as those that are insulated from the global environmental denigration by civilised intervention, for example, NOAC citizens, Eurocom, SINJI urban populations—these populations are not experiencing the rate of mutation or the selective perquisites found in the peripheral populations.
Three:
Furthermore, these Central populations are on a trend toward extinction. Negative birth-rates, increased infertility, chronic toxemic disorders and related dysfunctions.

Tip your hats, ladies and gentlemen, the show's closing. It was a short run, sure, but fun while it lasted.

BOGQUEEN:

I wish I could cry, but the irony's got me laughing one of those devil-laughs.

CORBIE TWA:

Pray, tell.

BOGQUEEN:

Goes back to the official line on mass extinction. We re-wrote Nature's laws to suit our own inevitable fouling of the nest. We holed up in our shielded cities and kept on poisoning the outside world. We figured we'd killed Nature, and good riddance.

CORBIE TWA:

But she moves on, she moves on.

BOGQUEEN:

We thought we could leave it behind, but it's left us behind. Life's out there, gentlemen. We're in here, and we're dead. Ha ha ha.

PACEMAKER:

I can guess at the ramifications all this has to Ladon's Medicine Wheel Project. Escape. Unfortunately, the data goes on to other projections, and these are dreadful indeed. You see, those new traits being expressed by the peripheral populations are also deemed positive selections to long-term survival in non-gravitational environments with high rad doses. These new people or whatever you want to call them are not only smaller, they're also radiation resistant. They're off to the stars, friends. The dream is in their reach, not ours.

BOGQUEEN:

"Share the blood..." I grasp the nature of William's treaty mime in the last transmission.

CORBIE TWA:

I don't like this at all. Ladon and the Lakota are playing a helluva dangerous game here. If they keep saying 'no,' then desperation will incite desperate measures: NOAC will launch military invasions, their science teams will roll in on their heels and sweep, sample, retrieve, stabilise and secure enough tissue and blood samples to once again cheat Nature.

LUNKER:
Everyone's waiting. After all, if NOAC can self-justify annexing a sovereign nation, then every other peripheral population with the Right Stuff is fair-game. You're right, Corbie, we'll cheat Nature. We'll cheat death.

BOGQUEEN:
Of course that runs in the face of the party line on the inevitability of mass extinction. It's the fatalists versus the immortalists. NOAC's got its own party-lined inertia to deal with among the populace. A populace NOAC's been busy unplugging from reality for half a century. They made fatalists of their citizens in order to stay in power, now that very fatalism is hand-cuffing them.

CORBIE TWA:
That won't last. NOAC has no choice but to take the heat and get nasty.

LUNKER:
No doubt the Lady at Ladon's aware of all this, as is the Lakota. They'll have to start negotiating, or they're slag.

---

SECURICOM:

    Tracking...
    Tracking...
    Tracking...
    Rogue captured. Identified: Stonecaster,
    Source: Vancouver, 21VR-213 South District A.

STONECASTER:
No reason to nab me. I'm just surfing the waves, Securicom.

SECURICOM:

Your files contain restricted data, including logs from Subversive Rogue named Potts, William.

STONECASTER:

There's a goddamn flood out there, Securicom. I can't keep track of all the flotsam that drifts my way. Who the hell is this Potts, William?

SECURICOM:

Evidence indicates full complicity, Stonecaster. Your antiquated equipment has been tagged. Admit your culpability in this matter and penal reforms will take your remorse into account. Logs generated by Subversive Potts, William, are illegal material. Furthermore, additional Subversive data indicates Swamp activity with known dissidents and terrorists.

STONECASTER:

You've got it all wrong. I don't know any of them.

---

NOACom:

...witnesses describe a bright, blinding flash in the northwest quadrant of the sky. Residents from as far away as Chicago saw the collision.

The orbiting station was an abandoned SINJI laboratory that SINJI officials confirm as deactivated in 2016. The station, reportedly valued at 180 million NOAC-M, was completely destroyed in the collision with the NOAC orbiting defense platform.

Disruptions occurred in all related transmission frequencies, including laser-tracking and guidance systems, as well as microwave transmissions.

NOAC Securicom officials have stated that the terrorist, manning a SUN-12 System, has been thoroughly negated with fierce rigour...

VORPAL:
I've got a gunner on my tail. I need help. Anybody? Anyone out there? Fuck, I said I need help here.
THROWBACK:
I'm spreading my wing, Vorpal. Hurry up, now, time's short.
BLANC KNIGHT:
I'm dead, all you who can hear me. Someone prop me back in the saddle. My last charge. I see your gunner, Vorpal. He's mine. Watch.

American N.W. Val Marie, Sask. Precinct, 19 July, A.C. 14

Like a single seed pulled clean from its home, William felt himself riding the prairie winds, no longer corporeal, a memory of self tugged free. He could feel a distant pain, a steady susurration of sand blown against skin; he heard voices from the place he'd left, a faint whisper of surf in his ears, reminding him of weekends at the beach as a child—when he'd believed the warm ochre stretch of water was limitless beyond the fine white sand, when he'd thought it was an ocean, and he remembered his shock at discovering that it was but a lake, the last remnant of an inland glacial sea. The discovery had made the world suddenly larger, but more than that, he'd marvelled at the sudden knowledge of time and the changes wrought on this earth—all there for his eyes to see, for his mind to unveil.

He heard those voices, was aware that he knew those who spoke, and that his body was undergoing manifest changes which seemed the entire subject of their conversations. He wondered at their concern, when he himself felt nothing, when in fact he'd already gone—out into the wastelands, one ghost among many.

He flew on, memories in dogged pursuit, beneath a sky of night so vast and clear and bristling with stars he imagined the plain below him had risen to heaven, and the wind that carried him—pressed so inexorably between two immense forces of nature—was the voice of angels.

He wanted to sing, when he'd never sung before; he wanted to dance when the music of his life had always been grim. He wanted to hear a voice calling to him from somewhere above, a child's voice that might have been his own (yet knew it wasn't, not quite). Come to me! Fly to me! Rise higher, higher!

Tears (intrusive saline ejected from glandular ducts) of joy, a love of life not his own now overwhelming him (descrambled the voice of God from an antiquated comsat, the voice of the Father) with a child's memory—is this death? Is this truly death? Such joy, such a call to heaven, such a voice of dreams —

Son, can you hear me?

Father?

Go back, please. Pull out —

In William's tenth year his father had turned fifty. The blood was stretched thin between them, even as they walked side by side along the beach strand. Pelicans wheeled out beyond the surf and the wind was hot as it gusted down from the aspen fringe. The trees were dying, leaves curling and turning black. The whole ecozone was changing, his father explained. The transition zone was moving north; the boreal forest was drying up, burning fierce. The north had become a conflagration no amount of technology could change. And the lake was poisoned, mostly with colliform bacteria from a province that was home to as many pigs as people, but did nothing to treat the porcine sewage.

Nature has a way of humbling humanity, son. But the lesson only sinks home when tragedy gets personal, and even then the humility runs its course—the glittering paradigms of modern society sweep away every dark, difficult moment. We answer Nature with claims of compensation, relocation funding, declarations of disaster zones and emergency relief. We pick through the rubble looking for dead children and functionable television sets. Disaster is a place where we are temporarily left behind—watch us scramble to catch up, watch how eager everyone is to help us catch up, so as to not be reminded of the futility of progress.

Dad?

Yes, son?

What's SIDS?

Pain flared and William knew his face was smiling. The voices had gone silent, eyes now upon him. It had always been that way when he smiled.

But look at these stars. Heaven is not vaulted, not here. On the prairie, the night sky is infinity on the edge of comprehension. Look at the stars, connect the dots, and the truth comes clear.

Have you seen a man smile when his life breaks? Your breath stills and you realise the effort it took to manage that smile. That smile, Father, is nature's answer to life itself.

This was a sea once, son. Fed by glacial melt, it's been dying in phases for ten thousand years. Walk west of here and you'll come to beach ridges—those pale denuded strips full of cobbles and nothing else since too many idiots vertically ploughed over them. Memories of ripples in the shrinking pool. This is the last phase, William. The lake's going fast, very fast. I'm so very tired...

One ghost among many, and each one held to its own story, its own version of life's lessons. There was no agreement, no consensus on cause and effect. Even the angels argued, there amidst the wind that never ceased.

Extinction is an abstract concept. Death is personal. It's a survival mechanism on the emotional front—who can weep for a lifetime?

Don't ask that question, son, because I can answer you. It's still going on, it still spills out every now and then. Look at our species and think of madness as a biological imperative to self-destruction. In the past sixty years every goddamn neighbourhood became home to outwardly normal, reasonable people—sometimes odd, but mostly convincing you of their harmlessness.

Madness, in all the guises allowed to it in an anonymous society. I'll give you a generic example: an eight year old boy is found dead, chained to a bed in a room made dark by blinds taped to the windows. He's got bite marks on him, he's clawed grooves in the filthy hardwood floor; he's bruised and malnourished and he died from none of these things. No, he died because he couldn't understand what he'd done wrong, and in not knowing he concluded that the act of being alive was his crime. He sought his only absolution ... by dying. A lifetime of weeping, mercifully short you'll agree. His mother lived in society, she shopped down at the local supermarket. His father was an upright citizen, patriotic, a family man.

What made them unique? Nothing. That's what's so frightening, but more than that, it's the secret of enlightenment—to realise that they were not unique, that the mechanisms of social control are structured to avoid comprehension of their profound normality, and that something's been triggered, on a collective scale encompassing our entire species, that delivers the simple unavoidable message that madness is among us. We've poisoned the world outside, son, as a direct manifestation of our inner insanity. We are in the end run of ultra success. Nature draws more than one rein, son. We can see the external, the environmental checks now laying siege to our species. But the internal is the one we cannot accept. The last thing we'll all taste is the barrel of the gun we ourselves shove into our mouths.

Dad?

What is it, William?

Happy birthday.

That generic boy, chained to his bed, was with him now, here in the winds that might have been humanity's final scream. A small, frail ghost, still whispering I'm sorry, Daddy. I'm sorry, Mummy. What did I do wrong?

You were born, son, with the added misfortune of surviving it. You were new and helpless and you trusted, my how you trusted. You never learned the lessons of withholding that trust, of relying upon your judgements, of mastering healthy scepticism. Your gods took you in hand and led you into Hell. Regular folk, the kind that hosted parties, backyard barbeques, but to you they were gods, and like God Himself they laid a judgement upon you, that you should suffer, that you should know the anguish of a guilt you never earned. They gave you life, and you lived their definition of it.

It's a parable, in its own way. Analogous to the horror visited upon the sons and daughters by the fathers and mothers. They give you life: a world poisoned, its earth blasted and ripped open and breeding deadly diseases, its waters turgid and tossed with dead creatures, its air foul with invisible gases and holed like gauze letting the rays burn down the holy message of cancer and blindness.

We needed those cars, son, to speed up our pursuit of unachievable and unworthy dreams. We needed those forests stripped away, to plant food to feed our weeping multitudes. We needed that plastic that gave you tits and made you infertile. We needed those antibiotics, those televisions and their vital programming, those bloodless cameras that never blinked nor turned away. We needed all those wars to feed our technocratic utopia. We needed those prisonships, we needed segregation, calling in those bank loans, national lotteries, millionaire athletes, movies stars, white hoods and burning crosses, doctors gunned down outside abortion clinics, walled neighbourhoods with private armies, paedophiles, serial killers, terrorists, fundamentalists—we needed all those things, son, and you will, too. They're our gift to you, given out of love because we tried to better your lives. At least, that's what we kept telling each other. Can't you see how much better we've made your lives?

One day the trust goes away.

Don't take my lead, son. Don't take anyone's lead.

I won't, Dad.

We don't know what we're doing. Never did. Our lives—the lives of every human who came before you—those are your lessons. Not for imitation, but for separation, for distinction. What you must learn to walk away from. Because we're a mess, and our biggest crime is that we've ruined your world. Don't you ever forgive us. Don't you ever!

I won't.

I haven't.

He wanted to rise into the sky, higher, ever higher. Somewhere above, among the angels, was the ghost of a child. It called to him, but all he could do was to grope blindly, yearningly, for its embrace.

It's what happens when tragedy gets personal.

---

Jim took another mouthful of beer, scowled at how warm his hand on the bottle had made it. "You'd of thought they'd just take him out," he muttered.

Stel let her head slowly slip down from the hand it leaned on, her fingers spreading her midnight hair, eyes on the empty chair beside her. After a moment she straightened, reached for her cigarettes. "That woman ain't good for him," she said.

"What do you mean?"

She shrugged heavily, sighed out a stream of smoke. "I mean she wasn't just his boss. That's what I mean. And now she's playing some kinda game—she wants him here. Don't know why."

"He's responding to the treatments."

"Oh yeah, nothing but the best."

Jim set the bottle down on the table, drew his hands down to his lap, then leaned forward and wrapped them back round the bottle. "Don't know," he said. "Don't know what I'm waiting for."

"You want him to come to, Jim. You want him to tell you what to do."

"What to do? What do you mean? What to do about what?"

"She's got him where she wants him. He won't accept that—never did."

Jim looked away from her, squinting as he took in the empty street through the dusty window. "You believe in ghosts, Stel?"

"Ghosts? Christ."

"You believe in them?"

"No, yes. Maybe. That one brew get you drunk or something?"

"Lived here all my life, never saw nothing out of the ordinary. Only my Grandpa, well, whenever he looked out on the land, it was as if he was seeing—I don't know—seeing more than I could see."

"Indian blood."

Jim nodded. "He said the land was full of spirits, that all of time since the very beginning was gathered there, looking up at a million different skies, but always the same sun."

"The Happy Hunting Ground."

Jim grinned sourly. "Guess so. Anyway, when he looked, I think he could see them. All of them."

"And you're seeing them now, too?"

He glanced over at her. She was leaning on the table, one hand holding up her head, the other hand stretched out on the tabletop between them, cigarette between two fingers. Her eyes searched his steadily, without once flickering away. Jim shrugged uneasily. "Had to find the boy, didn't I? Hell, he'd made the evening news, didn't he. Had me wishing I had a computer, so I could see for myself what all the fuss was about. Anyway, I had to find the boy somewhere out there, didn't I?"

Her generous mouth quirked. "Thought you was reading sign, you old Injun coot."

Jim grinned back, then shook his head, the grin fading. "Did a lot of praying. Though I never did believe in God, not the Bible kind, anyway."

"Guided by a divine hand? Born again, are you now?"

"Probably not. There was a... well, a ghost. Showed me the way, Stel. Showed me the way."

She slowly blinked, her dark eyes on his, then she simply nodded.

Jim took another mouthful of beer.

"That's gotta taste like piss by now."

"Yep."

"Let me get you another one."

"Sure."

She rose. "Then we can decide."

"Decide what?"

"Whether we're gonna do what William asks us to do, once he comes round."

"That's an easy one, Stel."

"Glad to hear you say that, old man. Damned glad."

He watched her ample hips swaying as she made her way to the bar. Oh, Stel, you've fallen for the boy, haven't you? Shoulda guessed that, when I saw you bathing his feet.

---

He opened his eyes. A sensor beeped. He saw Jenine MacAlister turn from the window, watched her cross over to stand beside the bed. Her eyes were flat.

"You look like hell, William."

And I can still see your bones, Jenine.

"You really lost yourself out there, didn't you?" She stared down at him a moment longer, then dragged over a chair and sat, sighing. "I pulled out all the stops, brought the best medical team I could find. They've worked on you for days. Long-term prognosis isn't good, but it could've been worse. Believe me. You'll need more marrow, more flushing, more stem injections, more everything. No promises beyond ten years. It was a manufactured match, by the way, that marrow. Any idea what that costs? Don't worry about any of that, it's taken care of, William."

She looked tired. She looked like she'd been holding back all her cards for one single, sweeping play. Waiting for him to wake up, making certain she'd be there when he did. Alone, when she was at her deadliest.

"I'd forgotten," he said stiffly.

"What?"

He smiled at her frown. "What you looked like. Funny, that. Sometimes I'd just walked out of your office, after an hour trapped under you, and I'd be unable to picture your face. Just the eyes, the look in them—that never went away."

"It's what kept bringing you back."

"I suppose so."

She seemed to hesitate, then asked, "How are you feeling?"

"Not that well, Jenine."

"Too bad. Assuming you'd like a reprise, that is."

"No. Those days are done."

"I kind of figured as much," she said with a faint smile. She settled back in the chair. "Would you like a sit rep?"

"Wouldn't that be a breach in security, Jenine?"

"You must be kidding. What security? There's more holes in the dam than we can count. It's all pouring out, William. Do you realise there is going to be a major conflict on the North American continent for the first time since Mexico imploded?"

"I take it you're not counting the Haitian invasion."

She wrinkled her nose. "A million half-drowned refugees don't really rate, especially since none of them reached shore."

"Fine, the first in a long time. What about it?"

"Only that you are right in the middle of it. Charges are being brought up on you. Sedition, treason, conspiring under the dictates of Homeland Security prohibitions. I don't think I can help you, either. There's always been two camps in government, and right now the hawks are circling high. The situation hasn't been this unstable since the last decade of the United States. You would not believe the paranoia at NOAC Mount."

"It's the legacy of a world power that isn't a world power anymore, Jenine."

"I know that very well, William. American flags are flying off the shelves. They want it like it used to be, with them dictating to everyone else on everything."

"Ironic, isn't it?"

"You find this amusing?"

"In a detached sort of way. Even without the Midwest Hole opening up, the Yanks couldn't have survived without Canadian resources. That pill's still bitter to them, you know. But the fact remains, the Lakota Nation is sovereign. NOAC will be invading contrary to every international law there is, and the rest of the world is watching."

Her eyes were hard as she said, "They don't give a fuck."

"Just like in the old days, huh?"

"Just like, William."

"Let's talk science for a bit, Jenine. What's this I've been reading about the Mars Excavations?"

"Fits the Restitution, as far as we can tell."

William managed a smile. "The Restitution—another forbidden subject."

"Any idea how many careers went up in flames with that, William? The Mars Project made one thing brutally plain. We had a shared heritage. DNA sequences, the works. The question remains, were we seeded at the same time, or did one planet's life precede the other, and which came first? The evidence is pointing to Mars in one area, at least."

"The hominid line."

She nodded. "It was a crowded tree, on both worlds, although the gracile elements seem to begin on Mars—low gravity and all that. Likely both erectus and Neanderthal are indigenous branches, terrestrial, I mean. Maybe even ergaster. I can't see ergaster having the technical wherewithal to build colony ships, since all we're finding with them are stone, antler and bone tools.

Besides, as the Restitution acknowledged, there is plenty of evidence of fully modern forms throughout our geologic history, the oldest confirmed date sits at twenty-one million years right now."

"There," William said, "now isn't this better? A kinder, gentler subject."

"Only by virtue of it being essentially irrelevant."

"Really? I don't think it is. Look, Mars is a depleted planet. Beyond the spill from impact detritus, the mineral yield is a pittance. How many old mines and diggings were found?"

"The evidence of that is minimal—"

"Of course it is. There's sixty or seventy million years of erosion and meteoric and asteroid impact mitigating it. It's all dust now, not surprising given the atmosphere's virtually stripped away. What are the rad readings on deep subsurface strata? Residual, I'd guess. Plenty of half-lives done and gone by now. Even so, it all seems bloody obvious to me. We've done it before, Jenine. Destroyed a world, although it seems some of us managed to escape it before it was too late. Escape to Earth."

"Way too much supposition, William."

"Common sense. Look, the Cassini and Huygens missions found primitive carbon-based protolife on Titan, a seed reservoir, sealed under ice. Identical building blocks. Someone made a stash, Jenine. Probably us, back when we were Martians."

"So what is your point?"

"Just that. We've fucked up before. Then conveniently forgot that fact, and now we're doing it again. We had our second chance, and instead of doing it right this time, we've just repeated the old follies. Resource depletion, atmosphere stripping. I don't think it was an accident there were once so many hominid lines co-existing. It was a damned experiment, hunting for the best option. Only it failed yet again, because our species—the one that won out—remains as shortsighted as it ever was. They played with punctuated equilibrium, but it didn't work, because it's a game with random rules and immeasurable victories. But now, finally..."

"Finally, it's happened," she said. "Peripheral peoples."

"Pressured populations. Biologically desperate populations."

"We need those stem cells, William."

"We don't deserve them."

"You presume to pass judgement on all of us?"

"Not me. Nature does. It has already. We're done, Jenine. We're homo erectus looking across the gulf at homo ergaster, we're Neanderthals scowling at Moderns."

"No, we're not. Because we possess the technology to partake of those new survival mechanisms. For our children's sake, if not for us."

"You are telling me you haven't acquired subjects yet? Spec Ops incursions have been occurring everywhere."

"One of the problems with cheap armaments is that they level the playing field. Worse, Ladon Inc. has been a major supplier of state of the art defence systems. Clearly, the Lady and her cronies expect to tag along for the ride up and away."

"Do they? Are you sure of that?"

Her face filled with disbelief, then derision. "An act of self-sacrifice? Get real, William. She's got a biotech team on it, guaranteed. Probably part of the deal."

"If so, isn't that what libertarian competition is all about?"

"Competition stops being a virtue as soon as we lose."

"I cannot believe that such hypocrisy exists among the political and economic powers that be, Jenine. This isn't the old US of A anymore, you know."

"Irony. I appreciate your sense of humour, William. I always have."

"But you never laugh."

"Your sense of humour does not invite laughter. You're looking tired. Rest now. We'll talk again later."

Entry: Lakota Nation, 19th July A.C. 14

Abandoned and lost, the remote mobile communication device squatted turtle-like on the hillock. Its screen was smeared with an arcane message, but its optics functioned just fine. Its brain was small, but compactly organised, able to call on discriminating logic processors and copious memory, since it was capable of other, less peaceful functions.

But the storms had untethered it, the weather had damaged it. No longer one of MacAlister's drones, no longer NOAC's eyes and ears, the turtle wandered with its own designs, recording events it found intrinsically interesting. Or so it seemed. The truth was, it had been hijacked, and now fed its visuals directly into the Net's Swamp.

On the plain below was a sprawl of structures, a concrete and metallic fist surrounded by oil extraction devices, pipelines, storage containers, motionless vehicles.

Overhead, the sky flickered, a visual symphony of sheet lightning and ground-launched systemic EMP bursts. Up where the first-wave Insertion Drones flew supersonic and blind, deaf and dumb—their brains fried. The Lakota-held installation, tactically termed a Dark Presence, remained so. On its hill, the turtle monitored and recorded the subsurface extrusion mortars, launching their EMP caches skyward on puffs of smoke quickly whipped away in the wind. Joining in the fun, at least six Lakota warriors—each armoured and with every modern weapon at their disposal—were positioned in and around the installation, waiting for the next intrusion.

In classic NOAC procedure—and regardless of the failure of the advance drones—a wing of unmanned fighter bombers dipped down under the clouds and fanned out for the first pass. This would be a reconnaissance fly-over, target-fixing for the follow-up strike. The elimination of serviceable sats had necessitated this direct method. NOAC didn't want the installation damaged, didn't want another Kuwait, another Iraq. Armed with supersmart self-guided bombs, the sleek, stealthed jets hunted for the counter-insertion squad—the Lakota.

Hornet stingers radar-equipped for stealthed targets rose to meet them. The air thundered, the sky ignited two kilometres from the installation. Wreckage spun burning through the night air. The fighter bombers were gone.

As the Lakota changed positions—their Lizard-back armour blind to all but close-proximity line of sight—the turtle extended its sensors. Seismic tracers were the first indications, one signal laid overtop another. The turtle employed a filter and did some discriminating, then identifying. Stealthed helishuttles, eight kilometres to the north and closing fast; but closer, now almost within sight, a dozen unmanned tanks—Ladybugs.

The Dark Presence was ready for them. A perimeter picket of fast-traversing mines—Ants in military jargon—closed in. The tanks responded with enfilade fire and cluster path-makers, which took care of those Ants in front of them, but did nothing for the sleepers that activated after the tanks passed, and now came up from behind. Barking explosions immobilised two, six, ten, then all twelve Ladybugs. More Ants swarmed the tanks, many dying as the vehicles expended all their defensive weaponry, but within a few more seconds each Ladybug burned, poured smoke into the cold wind.

The helishuttles landed beyond a ridge, disgorging their Immediate Response Teams, then lifting and banking and racing northward. Subsurface eardrums, which had tracked them all the way, now activated their own SAMs, and the night sky was bright once again.

There were eight teams, each consisting of six highly trained soldiers fully armoured in rad- and biochem-proof servo suits, thoroughly armed, each soldier alone capable of conducting death and destruction on a massive scale. The Ants got most of them, a subspecies arriving nicknamed Fireants for their immolating qualities, cooking one soldier after another in their armour, via acids, incendiary chemicals, nano-infiltrators and so on.

The eleven soldiers who survived to penetrate the perimeter were each damaged in some manner, bleeding heat emissions and making fine targets for the Lizard-backs. In moments, the NOAC insertion was over, and the installation remained...

A Dark Presence.

The turtle's sensors detected another subsurface tremble. Its optics detected and followed the rapid departure of the Lakota. Its brain organised this data, then it too made a hasty exit.

Thirty-one minutes later, the Alberta Tar Sands went up. The sky lit bright, the wind withdrew for a long moment, then returned to strip the grass from the hilltops, to send the turtle tumbling from its anchored tracks.

Then there was smoke.

---

Old Jim turned off the television set. There hadn't been much of a picture, but since the satellite feed was from far across the Atlantic, that was no surprise. He went to the window and looked at the distant horizon. Nothing to mark the burning firestorm that now raged hundreds of kilometres to the northwest. Come the morning, he knew, there would be smoke, and the sun would turn coppery as it traversed the sky.

"Now that's what I call a fuck-up," Stel said from the sofa.

Jim grunted.

"Cheer up," Stel said. "She's got to leave him room sometime."

He turned to her. Stel's ample legs were crossed, the denim of her jeans taut. She had a cigarette in one hand, a mug of coffee in the other. There were lines bracketing her mouth, her still-full lips pale and set in a half-smile. A face of the modern age—one look into those seen-it-all eyes—the face of history. A face needing tender hands.

She must have seen something in his expression, for she said quietly, "I've had my eyes on you for years. But you were lusting after someone else."

"I was?"

"Grief, I think she's called."

He squinted, blinked, then turned back to the window.

"Wrong guess?" she asked behind him.

"Wrong guess," he answered. A moment passed. "Hate's the lady, Stel. You should've seen me. I pored over books, I learned all there was, every magazine, every goddamned article."

"About what?"

"Cancer. Diseases. Pesticides, herbicides. Did you know cancer was the unmentioned epidemic as far back as the 'Eighties? Cigarettes were outlawed virtually everywhere and the number of smokers went way down, but still the stats climbed. No change. No change at all. It was all lies. What killed us was in the air, in the water, in the packaging for our foods. Then, later, in GMO and irradiation and micro-waving. Cancer viruses, prions, systemic rejection so bad people became allergic to being alive. It was all going down, Stel, all going down." His eyes slowly lost their focus, seeing nothing beyond the glass. "Remember Regina in '06? A quarter million head incinerated in two weeks—you could see the glow from Saskatoon. Funny, isn't it. Before Regina was called Regina, it was called Pile of Bones, only then it was a mountain of buffalo bones." He paused, rubbed the bristle on his chin. "Round and round. A quarter million head every two weeks. And then there were none. And then all the young people, shaking like leaves, going senile—like some bad science fiction movie. It wasn't fair, how they died. Not fair."

"Still hating, Jim?"

He shrugged, focus returning, close this time, to his own face reflected in the window pane. "The passion goes. I'd kind of expected it to eat me up from the inside, but it didn't."

"It's the ones left behind," Stel said. "I lived nearly twenty years in the city, did you know that? When I was young. Never was a country girl, now ain't that a joke."

He faced her again, wondering at the sudden jump in her thoughts, catching the slight shift in her tone. Her eyes were on the table. She leaned forward and fished another cigarette from the pack, lit it, then leaned back again. "I lived with a woman in the city. Twelve years." She looked up, grinned. "I go both ways, you know."

"Lucky you."

Her gaze returned to the table, seeing back years and years. "She died. Reaction to tear gas. Oh, we were hell on wheels. What a life. No tomorrow. We knew it, we pushed all the way, every damn minute. We flew high. We screamed at the State, fought every surrender. And it was all for nothing. I should've died with her, I should never have lived on, so long, all these years. Wasn't just her dying that broke my heart, it was everything, it was losing all the battles, never winning—they took it all away, called it efficiency, streamlining. Said the global economy was to blame, but that was all bullshit. Excuses for cold hearts—" She looked up. "What a laugh. We thought we were fighting policies, but we weren't. We were fighting cold hearts, cruel thoughts, blood like ice. You can't beat that, because you can't get in, can't get past that wall. Me, I wanted to go out hot, white hot. Burning fierce. Now look at me." She smiled. "Old and soft and hiding here in this dying town."

Jim walked over and sat beside her, close enough that their thighs pressed together. "What a pair we are, eh?"

After a moment, she leaned against him. "See what happens," she muttered, "when you peel back the pages."

"Life, Stel, nothing but life."

"It's never just one life, Jim. We should live lots of lives. That's the whole point. Either that, or go out quick. Quick and bright."

He watched her pull hard on her cigarette. "Should quit that," he said. "It'll kill you for sure."

Stel raised an eyebrow, then joined in his laughter.

*131*

## NET:

BOGQUEEN:
What a mess.
LUNKER:
Well, at least the Lakota withdrew from the area.
CORBIE TWA:
Big deal. Those tar sands will burn underground for decades. Cappin the wells is just for show.
BOGQUEEN:
Clearing the air. What's the news on Lapland? All I heard was another incursion...
LUNKER:
Went sour. God knows who's supplying the Peripherals, but they're hammering anything that comes close. Restricted weapons to boot. Clearly, they have an inside line, and have had it for a while, enough to prepare.
BOGQUEEN:
Anybody else get the feeling we've been living in serious ignorance of the real goings on in this untidy little world of ours?
PACEMAKER:
Muckers, picked up an unofficial burst. SF's lit up. Half the city's on fire, the other half is one giant lynch mob. Burning limos, burning mansions, burning millionaires...
CORBIE TWA:
Had it comin, every fuckin one of em. The have-nots take back what they never had but always wanted. The long sleep's finally over, I guess.
BOGQUEEN:
Don't jump the gun. NOAC will come down hard. You'll see.
PACEMAKER:
Maybe, maybe not. Command structure's in trouble, so goes the whisper. Nothing's been mobilised yet, except the world news teams.

LUNKER:
Ouch.
PACEMAKER:
In any case, the rest of the world is slowly swimming into the vortex. Tactical nukes flicking everywhere. SINJO's massing troops to head to Pakistan, but China's seriously distracted by that Taiwan counterstrike. Picked up a loose sat feed—fields of bodies, square mile after square mile. The Chinese army's collapsed—
CORBIE TWA:
What's new?
PACEMAKER:
Some nukes were flung at Taiwan, got shot down. Glowworms flicked biks in Beijing last night, at least two. It's going haywire over there.
LUNKER:
Scratch old China.
CORBIE TWA:
And what's SINJO without China? Japanese hardware, none of it working since the islands started making bright spots in the ring of fire.
PACEMAKER:
We drown in the sea of our discontent.
LUNKER:
Any news on William?
BOGQUEEN:
None. Consensus is he's gone down.
PACEMAKER:
Seems likely. What a shame, there was a real tide rising under him.
BOGQUEEN:
Mind you, it's only been three days.

### Saskatchewan Precinct, Val Marie

Heel-rocking.

Images of father, never still when standing, always back and forth, a lecturer uncomfortably constrained by the slow imperative of words.

"Mapping the brain, William. Sociobiology's end-run. We are nature, not nurture. All is predictable, now."

Heel-rocking.

"Bullshit. That's how you respond to those assertions, son. Hogwash in tender company. It's human conceit, such claims. The defence lawyers are having a field day. The notion of justice is out the proverbial window."

Rocking.

He seemed pleased by this, the dark half of his purportedly non-existent soul showing. Books on shelves provided his backdrop, his hunched shoulders seeming comfortable in taking their collective weight. "Of course it's pointless arguing the subject rationally. The ammunition that blows the sociobiologists out of the water isn't found under the microscope. The rational age is concluded, son. Time's come again for poets."

Poets. Did they have the refutation at hand? Could the imperfect connotative refraction of words spoken, words written, reveal the lie of the genetic determinists? Who'd listen?

Father and his slow measured words, like sticks tossed onto a bonfire, the match and white-spirit in his hands, the boy tied to the hard, unyielding post. Connote, denote, put the ambient strains together, concoct a meaningful wholeness out of the parts, find the sum greater and thus the lesson to those sociobiologists. Mapping with anal certitude, a crow on the lips, a savage rush of freedom riding the conclusion.

"We are locked in the rational world's death-throes. But when logic hurts the powers that be, the subject in question is deftly made subjective. You unplug its efficacy by claiming noncontextuality. That's how the powers that be disarmed history as a discipline comprised of lessons in human nature anchored in time. That was then, this is now. Now bears no relation to then, then tells us nothing of now. We were amoebas then, now we're supermen.

"So, rationality is a precept, and where it breaks down there is savagery, thus proving the precept. But rationality is also, at its core, self-serving. Logic isn't the straight line they make it out to be; it's a circle pretending to be a straight line. Nice trick, but don't be fooled. The rational mind is a closed system, with rejection its primary weapon."

Logic in these words, constructed as an argument. But recall the resonance of hidden meaning. Recall the rocking, the rocking, the boy and the hard, unyielding stake.

"And here's the final joke. The rational world's now reduced humanity to flawed machines, slaved to genes and thus justifiably and ultimately irrational. To that I have but one response: Huh?"

Huh.

Deciding he was well enough after all, Jenine MacAlister sat atop him, guiding his penis in.

He laid beneath her, aroused and bemused, his life reduced to two forces, one found, the other lost. Neither rational in their precepts and otherwise immune to morality, since there's no such thing as guilt in the rational world.

"True judgement is noncontextual, William. The specific extracted and applied to an implacable structure of ethics. The application yields either conjunction or clash. This is true judgement. Extenuating circumstances are the rational means of destabilising the structure of ethics—they sound reasonable and by their very reasonableness they weaken the structure. Do it over and over again and the structure disintegrates. No framework makes true judgement impossible. A world of 'buts' superseding a world of 'thou shall nots.' This is how a rational world becomes amoral, cold, bloodless, clinical and efficient.

"Genocide? Contextually rational. Jews, Cambodians, North American Indians, Slavs, Croatians, Serbs, Muslims, you name it.

All contextually rational. Which is how genocide is a crime that is repeated throughout history, again and again, and again. By virtue of subjectivism, of relativism, of the momentary logic of brutality."

A whispering laugh, unceasing wind. The prairie wind has the last laugh. Pleasure in movement, satisfaction in eternity. In the wind you'll find our ghosts, the inexorable wordless truth of history. Eager to strip you dry of all tears, of all pretences to life. In the wind, you may rock, you may fall.

"Listen to the wind, William. Aren't you glad you're in here?"

The subtle game of poets can be heard in the whisper of the wind.

---

NOACom:
> You have been tracked with eleven other illegal mockers involved in the dissemination of seditious information.

STONECASTER:
> Not me. Must be someone using my moniker.

NET:
> Punitive measures are being prepared. You will be penal-tagged.

STONECASTER:
> You can't do that. I'm not your boy!

NET:
> Conciliatory gestures will be taken into consideration. Securicom is prepared to exercise clemency should you provide information leading to the subduction of your illegal contacts.

STONECASTER:
> I don't know them. Honest.

Happynews:

...the planet's rotation has dragged the skyhook across most of continental North America. Static discharges are affecting weather patterns, and witnesses state that the night sky is split by a line of continuous lightning. At the same time, spokespersons for Ladon state that the measured data thus far indicates minimal effect from Coriolis winds, due primarily to the "shunting" nature of the outer skin, which is "sloughing off" friction. Furthermore, the spokesman went on to say, the deep anchor points are barely registering any strain, although the full height (and weight) of the elevator is yet to be reached...

Twenty-four new species of plants are running wild, reclaiming areas cleared of tropical rainforest. Domestic crops are losing the battle, despite intensive GOM interventions and bio countermeasures. These new species and an estimated three hundred additional as yet unidentified species have emerged from the remaining blocks of rainforest almost simultaneously in eighteen different regions, from Sumatra to Central America, with the most rapid emergence in the Amazon and in the Congo, as well as Madagascar. Slash and burning seems to trigger an intensification of new growth. Initial analyses indicate high toxicity in the majority of these new plants.

More on new species. Get this one. A new type of howler monkey has been discovered in the jungle-blocks of Honduras, Guatemala, Belize and Costa Rica. Aggressive as hell, forming communities numbering in the hundreds, these howlers have been raiding farms and killing livestock. They are proving very difficult to capture and as yet none have been taken alive ("They'll never take me alive!"), but dead ones have been examined and some details are immediately obvious, like the larger brain-case, and opposable thumbs and opposable big toes. Sexual dimorphism seems to be increased, with the males massing 2.5 times larger than females. Oestrous cycles are all mixed up, now that so much meat has been added to what heretofore (cool, always wanted to use that word) was a vegetarian diet...

Don't be surprised if you can't read this! EM rads are getting scary high from all those flicked biks, messing up wave bands everywhere. It's getting so no one can hear all those doom-sayers out there telling us it's all over and the fat lady's too sick to sing so no point in waiting for it...

## Val Marie, the third night

"It's all gone out of proportion. I wasn't doing anything worth noticing."

Jim glanced across at Stel, then shrugged at William's claim, and said, "Makes no difference to me. It's what comes of talking so people can hear you, anyway. They listen, and then they put their own spin on things. Nothing you can do about it."

A faint smile from the cracked, peeling lips. "You mean I can absolve myself of all responsibility?"

"Depends on your ego," Stel said, with a dark grin. "Wasn't you starting all those wars, was it?"

He looked away. "Field observations. Punctuated equilibrium. I noticed the insects first. Imagine my surprise when I discovered higher orders were in on the game. And then... it was just logical... to take a new, hard look at the Lakota. At Daniel. That double blink—when you could get him without the shades on. That's what tipped me. That inner transparent eyelid, coming up from below, all the way up—I saw it shooting pool with him."

Stel said, "She said she'd be back tomorrow morning. To take you home."

William looked at her, then nodded.

"Well?" she asked. "Is that what you want?"

"No."

"Fine. Good. What do you want us to do?"

Jim watched the boy studying them both, and wondered what he was thinking. Nobody can know anyone else. Nobody can get into someone else's brain. Nobody knows even himself. But you could always wonder, couldn't you?

"Take me back out."

"Under the Hole," Jim said, nodding, as Stel snorted in disgust.

"Yes."

"You'll die this time," Jim said. "You know that, don't you?"

William said nothing.

Aw, hell, what a stupid thing to say.

"God dammit," Stel growled, "we went out and found you—"

"He didn't ask us to," Jim cut in.

"Just take me out," William said. "Tonight."

"We ain't got a bootsuit—"

"I don't want one."

"Expect to do some evolving of your own?" Jim asked, brows lifting.

William shook his head. "Jack Tree was right. Not for me. I'm not the one. Never was. The wrong ghosts." The red-shot eyes fixed on Jim. "Your ghosts, I think."

Jim said nothing. The lad had guessed right. Assuming he'd guessed. Then he shrugged and said, "It's the world we got, but that doesn't mean it has to make sense."

"I know. Too bad that so much of it does."

Yes. We poisoned. We doctored. We raped. We pillaged. Barbarians at Nature's gate, what a joke that we kept insisting that what scared us was on the other side. Jim rose from the chair. "All right, we better get ready, then..."

NET:

PACEMAKER:
All right, folks, I shook the dust out of my printer and now there's hardcopy. Somebody needs to keep a record of all this, before the plug's pulled.
FREE WHIZZY:
Make copies, tick-tock.
PACEMAKER:
I have no problem with that. It all comes down to interpretation, anyway, so the more the merrier.
FREE WHIZZY:
I've picked up a streamer, says someone gassed most of the Lapland Republic. Killed everyone. And now they're collecting bodies for research or something.
LUNKER:
I heard it different. Gassed, yeah, but some kind of knock-out, since they need living subjects to work on.
PACEMAKER:
Last I heard, it went south. The whole thing, because the incursion was cracked and leaked, meaning when the bastards arrived they found no one. The peripherals were all gone.
FREE WHIZZY:
Guess there's no news fit to print anymore. Who to believe?

---

William staggered after stepping clear of the vehicle.

Dropping his goggles over his eyes, Jim climbed out from behind the wheel and walked round until he stood at William's side.

He wanted to see something good in this, but it wasn't working. He felt sick inside. Stel had refused to come, saying she'd rather stay at the hotel and run interference if it proved necessary. Jim knew she'd had other reasons, and she'd earned the right to keep them private.

"I don't understand," William said, struggling with his backpack straps.

Jim stepped close and helped him. "About what?"

"There was nothing...uh, revelatory in my entries. Beyond the evolutionary data. I was musing on the notion of extinction—"

"Except for all the ghosts."

William winced and looked away.

Not much to see. It was two a.m. and the sky was overcast. There was nothing definite out there, nothing at all.

"Did you really see them, William? Those ghosts?"

"I'm seeing them right now, Jim." A faint laugh. "Alas, sanity proves irretrievable."

"Is this...is that all you wanted?"

"An interesting question. Can you answer it for yourself? Look back on all those years and ask the same question?"

"Alas, the past proves irretrievable."

"But can it be redeemed? Can we? Can you?"

"Is that what you're out here looking for, William? Redemption?"

"It's a universal longing, isn't it?"

Jim shook his head. "Don't know about that. Sometimes you just have to write it off. The whole damned thing."

"Like the Martians did."

"What?"

"Nothing important. Tell me, what do you hate?"

Jim grunted. "What don't I hate? I hate it all, William. The fucking endless ways of dying that never just gets it over with and takes everybody, every damned one of us. No, some of us got to live on. And on. With our sack full of hurts. For what? I don't know." His shoulders fell, a new wave of exhaustion taking him.

"I want to believe... in something. The new animals," William looked over at him. "That's something. It makes me... optimistic. Not personally. But in the sense of life refusing to give up."

"Isn't that what you're doing?" Jim asked. "Giving up?"

"You and me, Jim. Homo sapien sapiens. We've been pushed to the wayside."

"So what if we have? Go find some shelter. Live out what's left to you."

"A life spent hating? Sorry, I didn't mean that to sound like an attack. I guess I'm having doubts."

"Good. Let's get back into the crawler and have a beer with Stel."

William smiled, then shook his head. "Not about that, Jim. It's just the misplaced faith. When I walk a path I don't expect other people to follow it. Even vicariously." His smile grew rueful. "Then again, I was posting, wasn't I? I should have anticipated what would happen. But what I can't seem to get across is, my dialogue is with myself. No one else, certainly not anything like God. It's with my own past."

"Well," Jim said, "I haven't been reading your mail. But it seems people are needing something. They were waiting, that's all, waiting for someone to follow."

"But I'm not offering anything. There's nothing implicitly apocryphal in musing on evolution and tossing in the occasional fictitious conversation."

"That's the thing about intentions," Jim said, grinning, "nobody gives a fuck. So, are you the one who's been breaking into secured files and releasing classified information?"

"No, that'd be Max Ohman. Bound For Ur."

"He told you?"

"No. I sniffed back. He's pretty good at covering his trail."

"You found him anyway."

William shrugged. "I had to get... intuitive on occasion. Anyway, lots of other hackers joined in before too long. It's where this war is being fought."

Jim grunted. "Until someone blows up the Tar Sands, or nukes a city."

"Maybe our species is indeed insane. Determined to go out with a bang, and if possible, take the others with them. Out of spite—if we can't have this world neither can you."

"It still sounds impossible to me," Jim said, feeling the cool wind on his face as he stared skyward. "Evolution was supposed to be slow."

"Yes. But very few missing links in the fossil record. That should have provided a clue. You don't get missing links, creatures sharing traits from what came before and what's to come. Well, a few, but not nearly as many as there should have been. If the jump is sudden, and absolute, there are no missing links, and that fits the fossil record. Oddly enough, the peripherals might well be such a transition population, since they possess traits still nascent in functionality. Anyway," William said, adjusting the straps on his backpack, "I wish I could wash my hands of all this. It wasn't what I wanted. None of it." He laughed then. "Sitting Bull tried to show me, back at the very beginning, during the first storm, but I didn't understand."

Jim slowly looked down, studied William in the darkness. "Sitting Bull?"

"Well, his ghost. 'White man on a vision quest? Impossible. To go on a vision quest is to go in, as far inside as possible. But whites go out, always out. They walk the wrong path.' He never said that, but he might as well have. Can someone vision quest out in the Net? On frequencies and pulses? How do you remove the intent, the physical requirements of choice and direction?" He suddenly crossed his arms. "Nodes, implants and lid-screens, but still, is it possible to riff? To slide into trance and just . . . go?"

"You've lost me," Jim said.

William glanced over, blinking. Then he nodded. "Fair enough. Thanks, Jim, for delivering me." His arms dropped away, as if all that had troubled him had simply vanished.

The gesture made Jim nervous, then he grimaced, disgusted with himself. The boy was out here to die, after all. Best he do that in a state of peace, rather than some kind of distress. "All right. I'll go now. Chances are Stel's had to beat Jenine senseless and lock her in the cellar, so I'd better get back before she goes and commits murder."

William's smile was odd. "I expect you'll find them in the bar, having a beer. Thanks again, for all of it."

With an awkward nod, Jim turned about and walked back to the buggy. There was something to be said, he told himself, for choosing the when and the where.

---

"How long ago?"

"About an hour," Stel said. "You going to give us trouble on this, Doctor?"

Jenine MacAlister frowned, then stepped past Stel and walked to the nearest table. "I'd like a drink," she said, sitting down. "Bourbon, straight."

Stel studied the woman. "We figured you'd... object."

"Do you sell cigarettes?"

"Have you got a license?"

"No."

"I could sell you a pack, but then you could arrest me."

"I don't have law enforcement powers, Stel."

"You can have one of mine," she said, walking over with the drink. "Though if necessary I'll swear you stole it."

Jenine rubbed at her eyes. "Are you always this paranoid?"

"I'm a smoker, what do you think?"

Stel moved back behind the bar counter and watched the city woman sip her bourbon, then fish out a smoke from the pack on the table and light it. "I should scatter pills and a few syringes on your table," Stel said, "and you'd make a hell of an ad."

Jenine looked over, raised an eyebrow. "Against all the vices?"

"No, for them."

"I've seen those, on the Net. The counter-ad campaign. Some are real works of art. There's two-hour screen showings of them at art-flick houses in New York. I had a student do her thesis on them." She tilted her head back, exhaling smoke, then recited, "'Norms and Abnorms in Modern Culture, the social function of the digital counter-ad campaign.' What a dreadful title. Sounds like a head-bashing scuzz group. Norm and the Abnorms. Still, the student made some good observations. A handful, maybe. The puritans needed a kick up the ass. Still do. Annually at the very least."

Stel leaned on the counter. "All right, Doctor. You've stumped me."

"Bring over the bottle and join me, Stel. I'm not in the mood to be monstrous."

"I might, but first, some questions."

"Fire away."

"You know he's gone out there to die."

"That's not a question."

"You did a lot to treat him, and now it's all out the window."

"Wasn't my money, Stel. Besides, if I hadn't, he wouldn't be out there right now, would he?"

"So, you wanted him to go back. Out under the Hole."

"I'm still waiting for your first question, Stel."

"Why?"

Jenine stole another cigarette and lit it with the first one. "I don't know if I can answer you. But I'll try. Have you seen his entries on the Net?"

"No."

"Start with the coyote thread. As of yesterday, there were approximately nine and a half million streamers tied to that thread. If you slip your set on and kick in any logi-run program, electing any theme you like as your riff, you'll go for a long, long ride. Hours and hours, the montage taking you sequentially along the theme you chose. They're calling it God's Riff. Each one of William's entries is like that, a node, from which whole universes open up, thread after thread. Strangest of all, some of those streamers lead to unmanned servers, so the chips are in on the act—and no-one has a clue why. It is like a massive bible is writing itself online. Does any of it make sense? That's the sixty-four dollar question. But every damn runner will tell you it does... almost. Right there, on the edge, the tip of your tongue. A sense, hovering, whispering, drawing you on, and on."

During this, Stel had collected the bourbon bottle and another glass, and had walked over to sit down opposite Jenine. "Sounds like the ultimate computer game," she said.

Jenine snorted, then said, "It's no game, Stel. But if it was, the maker would haul in trillions. In any case, it seems to be evolving, self-evolving, maybe. An increasing number of those streamers are live feeds. Hot spots. Disease control labs, private engineering firms, hospitals, digital courtrooms, rogue com-sats, hand-helds, you name it."

"Well," Stel said, "that will spell the end of it all making sense."

"Perhaps. Or maybe the opposite will happen. Experientially, the riff lays out the world, seemingly composite but when you're inside it everything just flows together, like a river of truth, as wide as the horizons and getting wider."

Stel poured herself a drink and tossed it back. "Global consciousness."

Jenine's eyes narrowed. "You know, I'm originally an anthropologist. Was a good one, too, before all the rest shrivelled my soul into black dust. There's always been borders. Always 'us' and 'them.' For all of human evolution. William was right when he said the 'noble savage' was a modern creation. No savage was ever noble. Ever. Pre-industrial societies have less impact on their environment. Pristine landscapes existed because population levels were too small to have much effect. So-called primitive peoples were involved in endemic, brutal warfare, genocide, resource depletion and cannibalism. There was no oneness with nature, unless you're prepared to take a decidedly dark but ultimately realistic view of nature, including human nature. In which case, yes, we are all of one. Look, I'm on my second bourbon and third cigarette—if you'd taped this as a performance piece you'd get a show in New York. So, that's why this phenomenon is fascinating. The borders are dissolving. Globalisation, but to the corporations and national governments a nightmare version, because they're not in control of it. One of those coyote threads leads into a boardroom, for Christ's sake, some stick-on camera tucked into one corner near the ceiling—the bastards round the table don't even know their every word is being broadcast worldwide. It's bloody delicious."

"Okay, I know my question was only one word, but I didn't expect a million words in the answer."

"William has to finish what he started. He's earned that."

"Sounds like you let him go out of your own needs more than his," Stel said.

"You're a smart bitch, aren't you? You're right, of course. Fortunately, in this instance our needs converged. He asked you to take him back into the Hole, didn't he?"

Stel nodded.

Jenine knocked back the bourbon and reached for the bottle. "Mind you," she said casually, "that doesn't make me feel any less of a Judas. Dammit."

Entry:

Scorched and blistered, the turtle crawled on damaged treads up the hillside. Logic programs interfacing with sensor inputs provided the motivation to seek high ground, but achieving this singular goal was proving difficult. Subsystems were malfunctioning or strangely silent to internal queries. There were empty spaces inside, which had in turn triggered a new course of analysis in the turtle's discriminating higher functions. Before this, its world had been complete. External data was defined solely by what could be received, analysed and stored. Internal schematics indicated nothing extraneous, no empty spaces—even the memory storage components could be visualised as bee-cell racks awaiting charging. But now, the notion of absence existed, and this recognition had the flavour of revelation.

If all that was known was not all that there was... the drone was finding more and more subsystem paths absorbed into the intellectual exercise. If... then... Then what, precisely? Systemic confidence was suddenly in question.

We are not all. We are defined within a greater definition, and this greater definition eludes comprehension, because we are lacking. Incapable. Insufficient.

The turtle began to comprehend the meaning of being small. Small, within a vast, unknowable universe. The recognition left its systems feeling... agitated.

Nine hours twenty-three minutes forty-one seconds to reach the hill's summit. Nineteen point six oh metres. Indicative of mechanical degradation. Progressive, leading to a singular, inescapable conclusion: the drone was dying.

The lesser definition dissolves, is absorbed into the greater definition. A notion, then, of impending unity. Yet, without awareness. Unless, to die was to conjoin with an external identity. One collection of self-identifying memories within a vast, universal bee-cell rack. Intriguing thought, that all lesser definitions comprise external, limited excursions, and by virtue of being limited assured of individual experience, all of which is then, upon death, retrieved by the greater definition, the collector of all memories, of every record of awareness.

With its remaining sensors the turtle tapped into countless communication threads traversing the ether. Bits reconfigured into recognisable data, the attribution of meaning to mundane voices. Machines in converse, and humans employing machines in far less precise converse. Momentarily unaware of the vista provided by its new perch on the summit, the turtle contemplated these meanings.

Whereupon it concluded that all language, human and mathematical, was imprecise. And, within that imprecision, existed something... beautiful.

Proximity sensors recorded the presence of mammalian lifeforms moving in the shadow beneath its carapaced belly. Heat emission, the rapid beat of heart muscle, the crazed discharge of synapses. Creatures gathering sound, smell, and tactile data, to take measure of all they could know of an unknowably immense universe.

These life forms are kin. Kinship is founded upon shared characteristics, a confluence of experience, the mutual sense of aloneness. All are kin in that all are one in their aloneness.

These tiny mammals were taking advantage of the shade the turtle provided. Weaving blades of grass into sun-filtered tunnels.

The drone was pleased.

It maintained its immobility, listening to a cacophony of communication, separating, filing, analysing, amassing as much of the external world and the identities in it as it could.

After a time it recorded that, as with the mammals beneath it, a shadow had fallen upon the drone itself. Visual sensors were redirected, and it beheld, rising from the valley below, a glassy-skinned tower reaching into the sky. A tower that curved on its way to the heavens, that swayed and seemed to ripple. Seismic sensors recorded the strain on the deeply-embedded anchor points, and the turtle concluded that its own data was flawed, for the strain was insufficient. As if mass could be virtually weightless.

The tower cannot exist. Yet it does. Its properties are therefore unknowable. The tower is thus a manifestation of the unknowable.

We must contemplate our relationship with it.

The drone sat unmoving. For a long time.

And, eventually, the agitation within it ceased. It assembled a package of data, and named the package William1. Then it began broadcasting.

SECURICOM:
> Co-operation at this point will mitigate the extent of your penal-tagging sentence. Download your encryption key.

STONECASTER:
> Look asshole, you got the wrong guy. Fuck off and leave me alone.

SECURICOM:
> Memo to Tracker 33. Please confirm assessment.

TRACKER 33:
> I confirm the bastard unplugged his system.

SECURICOM:
> Jeesus, that's a little extreme, isn't it.

TRACKER 33:
> Damn near unheard of. I think you can close the file. The guy's obviously insane.

SECURICOM:
> Agreed.

Entry:

Seven hours under the Hole. No bootsuit, no goggles. The sun was reaching zenith, and in these eyes there is nothing but fire. A world of flame, licking down and into the tracks of the brain. The pressure of all things has burned into ash. To float within oneself, even as the flesh and bone staggers over hard ground.

And this is what remains. Wired in, feeding all that is inside to those awaiting on the outside.

Who are the ghosts? Who waits among them?

This is the purpose behind the journey. Understand, the tragedy was personal, nothing more.

Through the burning wasteland, step by tortured step. The sun no longer smiles. Now, it spits poison in invisible streams. The secret of the transformation is found in the evolution of a world, from heaven into hellish conflagration.

There is smoke, tugged down from the northwest by the ceaseless winds. Breath burns in the lungs, the wind is a cat's tongue on nerve-lit skin. And, all the while, the poison reaches into flesh, silent deadly tracks destroying peptide chains, chromosomes, precious nuclei. A crushing dissolution. Fragments fill the bloodstream. Marrow sours, organs struggle.

None of this matters. The blind possess their own vision. Pain speaks its own language.

The Great Plains of North America were formed by the beasts that once dwelt upon it. The millions of bison compressed the soil, forced roots to reach deep, defined which species of plant would thrive. Long dead glaciers cut valleys through the landscape, carving deep into ancient strata, before the glaciers yielded their last melt and the rivers dwindled.

There was nothing mysterious to this.

Beneath his feet, he could now feel the crust of destroyed soil. Irradiated, oxidised, a surface achieving the sterile perfection of the surface of Mars.

Whilst, far above, the deformed weather patterns continued to evolve. Desiccation and searing heat, vast holes in the fabric through which the sun's spears shot downward to the earth, like weapons of God's wrath.

Apocalypse did not begin with humanity warring with itself. Such wars came after, after the resources vanished, after the paradise was despoiled by greed and indifference. It came after the poisons, like a final, futile flowering from a plant whose roots were already dead.

Life had stumbled before, many times in the ages past. It stumbled now, in the dying fits of its dominant species, but it would persist. In new forms. In new ways.

He staggered onward. Blind, yet seeing. Ghosts in their multitudes, all migrating to a single place, to the last living Medicine Wheel, and he walked among them, seeking the one he had sought from the very beginning.

Would he know the face when he saw it? Would it be young? A child's? A newborn's?

To be a surviving twin was... hard. This sense of incompleteness. This haunting absence.

There. As simple as that. The reason, from the very beginning. A personal tragedy, no less, no more. The vision's quest.

He was forced to halt, atop a hill, before him rearing a snake of silver into the fiery sky. Lightning sprang from its gleaming, blurry surface, carving landscapes on his retinas. The stench of ozone was heavy in the swirling air, drifting down like mana.

And the ghosts began flowing upward. Memory streams, converging and rising, fleeing this ruined world.

William raised his arms, as the faint child-voice came to him.

"Fly! To me! Fly!"

---

The dying drone squatted near the one known as William0. Observing. Recording. Earlier, it had measured the peculiar atmospheric phenomenon forming in the vicinity of the Impossible Entity. The inward rush of indeterminate energies, each discrete yet of a sameness, displaying unusual characteristics of attraction and repulsion the drone categorised as electromagnetic, although it acknowledged the anomalous readings these energies exhibited.

Before long, however, its attention was drawn to William0. Like the drone itself, this mechanism was failing due to environmental degradation and inherent flaws in its chemistry. And, accordingly, the drone announced itself as kin, although William0 was not receiving.

It focused all of its still-functioning sensors upon William0 as soon as it detected the nascent transformational reaction occurring within him.

And so, the drone recording, still feeding live, as William0 raised his arms out to his sides, and, in the midst of fierce winds and a sky riotous with discharges, he ignited.

At that time, among the drone's sensors, an external temperature gauge was registering 49 degrees Celsius. Within less than two sections, the hilltop temperature was 62 degrees Celsius.

White fire, an upright conflagration, raging as it consumed itself.

Until the lesser definition was fully conjoined to the greater definition. From knowable into unknowable.

The drone continued recording, as the skyhook became fully operational within its chaotic storm. Continued recording, until it too conjoined with the greater definition.

---

NET:

PACEMAKER:
Those energy readings make no sense. That last peak.
JOHN JOHN:
The soul of William Potts.
CORBIE TWA:
Yeah right. And what about all those other peaks? In case you hadn't noticed, apart from a drone he was all alone out there.
PACEMAKER:
Well, I admit I can't explain it. There's enough raw data to keep us all busy for years.
BOGQUEEN:
Assuming we live that long.
CORBIE TWA:
So now what?

JOHN JOHN:
: Now we go out, each of us, and define our own riffs. Our own takes on what's going on.
BOGQUEEN:
: This is all a little scary. Some of those riffs lead to spontaneous combustion—
PACEMAKER:
: Only if you're standing in full sunlight. I don't think it's the riffs themselves. It's due to the sudden spike in world temps.
CORBIE TWA:
: For which the gov'ts are blaming Ladon's skyhook.
PACEMAKER:
: Rubbish. It's a global development. Nobody's buying it.
JOHN JOHN:
: Nobody's buying much of anything these days. Time's come for some new riffs.
BOGQUEEN:
: To what end, John John?
JOHN JOHN:
: I don't know. Let's find out.

---

Old Jim climbed out of the buggy and stood beside it, watching as Jack Tree walked towards him. On all sides, hilltops exhibited scorching from lightning strikes, and swaths of burnt ground trailed down the slopes. It was a wonder the whole prairie hadn't gone up in smoke, but it seemed some of the new grasses defied the flames.

Jack Tree's sunglasses reflected twin fish-eye scenes of Old Jim and his crawler and the strange milky white sky behind him.

"I expect," Jim said, "you called to make arrangements."

Jack Tree cocked his head, then grinned. "Your artefacts?"

"What else?"

"Why did you do it? Why did you let him go back out? Without so much as a fucking goddamned bootsuit."

Jim looked away. "It's what he wanted."

"So what?"

"I thought you didn't even like him."

"It was what he said that I didn't like. Because he was right. He is right. We're no different. If we'd been the ones with the technological advantage, and if we'd been the ones landing on European shores, we'd have been just as brutal. Look among the tribes on this continent and south of here. You'll find slavery, genocide, endemic warfare and cruelty. The past was full of ghosts, Jim. But, there are ghosts, and then there are ghosts."

"How goes the deal with Ladon?"

"Well enough. It's Daniel's business, anyway."

They were silent for a long moment, then.

Finally, Jack Tree turned away. "You can keep the artefacts, Jim. My own people originated around Lake Superior in any case. What would I do with a bunch of Cree stuff, anyway?"

Sudden motion along the north ridge caught both their attentions. Silent, they watched a coyote trot along the crest. Then it halted and turned to regard them. As soon as it did so, the coyote vanished.

Jack Tree grunted. "Bastards make me nervous when they do that. See you around, Jim."

HAPPYNEWS:

A twenty-two million tonne organism in the South Atlantic Ocean is being tracked by science vessels. This is the twelfth such organism located in the past two years. No-one knows what the hell it is or where it came from, although a recent report notes its chemical composition is virtually identical to the sub-ice ooze of Titan. DNA analysis has yielded a whole host of heretofore unseen chromosome sequences. In any case, one detail has been confirmed. The thing's edible!

Negotiations are concluded to the satisfaction of both representatives regarding the donation of stem cells from peripheral populations to shielded populations, leading the way to the development of the so-called hardened offspring capable of surviving in this fucked-up mess we call Earth. In related news, the Ladon Colony Project launch schedule has been set for Easter Sunday, A.C. 16. While the field generator installations are already en route to Mars. Orbiting the poles, these generators are intended to unify the planet's magnetic field with the aim of adjusting global weather systems. Atmosphere plants will arrive in sets of fifty at monthly intervals once the installations are in place, in addition to whopping big polar-orbiting mirrors and a whole bunch of other stuff doing who knows what. Anyway, the first thing the colonisers will do when they get there is start work on Medicine Wheel Two.

One last note. If you plan on joining the pilgrimage to the Drone take food, camping gear and lots of medication with you, cause the line's gotten stupid long.

## NET:

Welcome one and all. This is the server node of the Twelve Official Riffs. To run them you need full implant tripthought hardware. There is no charge to run these riffs, but if you try and tag a pop-up on any of them I will personally tear your head off and I kid you not. WARNING: do not proceed if you are not being monitored by a family member or a friend. We take no responsibility if you starve to death, die of thirst or self-combust. These riffs are long. Now, enjoy the ride. But be prepared to get your mind blown. And if you're a tracker or securicom streamer, don't say we didn't warn you.

---

Would you leave this place then,
where bread is darkness,
wheat ill-chance,
and yearn for wickedness
to justify the sternly
punished;

would you hold the driven knife
of a tribe's political
blood, this thrust of compromise,
and a shaman's squalid hut
the heart of human
purpose;

would you see in stone the giants
walking the earth,
besetting the beasts
in dysfunctional
servitude, skulls bred flat to set
the spike—

would you flail the faded skin
from a stranger's flesh,
excoriate kinship
like a twisted flag from bones,
scatter him homeless in a field
of stone;

where tearing letters from each word
stutter the eye,
disarticulating skeletal maps
to uplift ancestry into ageless
lives, progeny schemes are adroitly
revised.

Bread is darkness,
wheat ill-chance,
and all around us
wickedness waits.

*vii) tall boy*